She shuddered at the first touch of his lips

There was an unbearable sweetness that came from being touched by Jesse. Before he could move, before he could stop, Desiree wrapped her arms around his back, pulling him even more tightly against her.

His lips closed over hers gently, sweetly, and for a moment the earth ceased to spin. Warmth started in her belly, as her body came to life for the very first time. His mouth moved against hers once, twice, and the warmth became a burning she never could have imagined. She moaned softly and opened her lips.

And then it was over. Jesse was thrusting her away from him, his breathing harsh. "Desiree–"

"Shh." She reached up, her fingers once again resting against his mouth. "Don't beat yourself up over this. I was the one who kissed you."

Then she spun around and ran toward home, knowing–deep inside–that her life had irrevocably changed. It might take her a few years, but Jesse Rainwater was going to be hers. He just didn't know it yet.

Dear Reader,

It is with great joy and excitement that I write this, my first letter to you, about *A Christmas Wedding*. This is a story near to my heart, not just because it is my first (which would be reason enough) but because it takes place very close to my own home.

I got the idea as I was driving through central Texas one summer day with my entire family. We had just passed a Thoroughbred farm and my oldest son, who was eight at the time, was fascinated by the place. His questions prompted me research to help him find the answers, and that research hooked me on the idea of a book set in the Thoroughbred racing world.

And though I had the setting down right away, the characters were a little harder to come by. I wanted a tough-as-nails Thoroughbred rancher, but I wanted her to be a woman. Imagine, I thought, the struggles she would have as she fought for her place in a sport still dominated largely by men. Well, Desiree Hawthorne was born, and because she needed a hero as strong and sexy and smart as she was, so was Jesse Rainwater.

I've written a number of books since *A Christmas Wedding* and have loved all of my characters. But Jesse and Desiree are my favorite, perhaps because they have to fight so hard to find—and hold on to—each other in a world that is constantly shifting beneath their feet.

I've been a Harlequin reader for twenty years now, ever since my mother first stuck a Harlequin Romance novel in my hand after a fruitless trip to the bookstore, where I had read every young adult novel on the shelves. Therefore it is a huge thrill to me to have my first novel be a Harlequin Superromance book. I hope you enjoy reading it as much as I enjoyed writing it—drop me a line at tracy@tracywolff.com and let me know what you think.

Merry Christmas and a Happy New Year.

Tracy Wolff

A CHRISTMAS WEDDING

Tracy Wolff

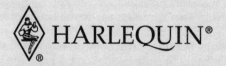

HARLEQUIN®

TORONTO • NEW YORK • LONDON
AMSTERDAM • PARIS • SYDNEY • HAMBURG
STOCKHOLM • ATHENS • TOKYO • MILAN • MADRID
PRAGUE • WARSAW • BUDAPEST • AUCKLAND

ISBN-13: 978-0-373-71529-9
ISBN-10:   0-373-71529-3

A CHRISTMAS WEDDING

This edition published by arrangement with Harlequin Books S.A.

® and TM are trademarks of the publisher. Trademarks indicated with
® are registered in the United States Patent and Trademark Office, the
Canadian Trade Marks Office and in other countries.

www.eHarlequin.com

Printed in U.S.A.

ABOUT THE AUTHOR

Tracy Wolff collects books, English degrees and lipsticks, and has been known to forget where—and sometimes who—she is when immersed in a great novel. Married for twelve years to the alpha hero of her dreams, she is the mother of three young sons and an English professor at her central Texas community college. Tracy loves to hear from her readers, so check out her Web site at www.tracywolff.com and her blog at sizzlingpens.blogspot.com.

For my mom,
who started this whole roller-coaster ride
so many years ago, and for Jenn, who swears
she always knew I could do it.
Thanks to both of you for sticking by me.

Acknowledgments

Beverley Sotolov for believing in this story and
for her patience as she helped a brand-new writer
get her feet wet so beautifully; and to
Wanda Ottewell for helping make this novel
the best it could be and answering
a million or so questions.
Thank you both.

CHAPTER ONE

"I'VE HAD IT, DESIREE. I can't do this anymore. Not for one more day. Not for one more *minute*."

"What's the matter?" Desiree Hawthorne-Rainwater asked with raised eyebrows, glancing up from her jewelry box just in time to see her husband of twenty-seven years hurl a large manila envelope at the center of the bed they hadn't shared in more than a year.

"This." Jesse's eyes darkened to obsidian as he used a sweeping gesture to encompass everything in the room, his voice vibrating with contained fury. "All of this."

Understanding moved through her, warming her for the first time in she couldn't say how long. At last, something they could agree on again.

The noise and chaos *were* grating—truck after truck of the supplies needed to make this afternoon and evening a success were arriving nonstop and she certainly couldn't blame Jesse for being annoyed by it when she herself had wanted to run away and bury herself in work more than once since this whole process had begun.

In a moment of weakness, she'd even contemplated offering Willow money if she would simply run away to Vegas—anything to get life back to normal on their idyllic Thoroughbred ranch in central Texas. But Willow had her heart set on a Christmas wedding—at home—and as mother of the bride and assistant wedding coordinator, burying her head and encouraging elopement hadn't really been an option.

"I know it's been crazy around here lately, but it'll settle down after the wedding this afternoon." She smiled wryly at the six feet, four inches of bristling, enraged masculinity currently regarding her with disbelieving eyes.

Part of her longed to reach a soothing hand out to him, but the tension between them had grown so thick in the past few months that she was afraid even that small gesture would rock the delicately balanced boat of their relationship. "We just need to hang in there a little longer."

"You think that's what this is all about? Willow's *wedding?*"

The warmth died as an icy trickle of unease moved through her. "Isn't it?" It was her turn to glance around the room. "Things are nuts around here today and have been for a while."

"You can't seriously be that out of touch." Jesse

shook his head, disgust evident in every line of his body. "If it would make Willow happy today, I'd gladly put on a gorilla suit and attempt to fly to the moon under my own power."

"Well, what, then?" She couldn't help the defensiveness that had crept into her tone—once upon a time he'd felt the same way about her.

"I'm talking about the new trainer you hired."

"Oh." Embarrassment washed through her—along with a healthy dose of annoyance. Hating the weakness her red cheeks hinted at, she focused on the annoyance instead. Fed it, until she was almost as angry as Jesse.

It wasn't as though she'd deliberately kept Tom's hiring from Jesse. She simply hadn't had time to discuss it in between all the other things going on the past couple of weeks. "I was going to talk to you about that."

"You were going to—" Jesse broke off in midsentence, his eyes narrowing dangerously—a sure sign that he was one small step away from total meltdown. He took a couple of deep breaths, then in a voice so quiet it hurt to listen to it, he asked, *"That's* the best you've got?"

Her irritation kicked into high gear. Who was he to question her decision—he who barely bothered to say three words to her at any given time? Who left a room almost as soon as she entered it? Besides, the Triple H was *her* ranch. *She* made the decisions on it and had for more than a decade and a half. "What do you want me to say, Jess? I did what I thought was best."

"Did you? I thought—" He broke off again. Rubbed a hand over his eyes. Turned away. When he finally spoke, his voice was devoid of emotion. "What you thought best. I guess that's what we're both doing, then."

He pointed at the envelope on the bed. "Sign the papers, Desiree. We both know this isn't working anymore."

"What papers?" she demanded as he stalked to the door. "Jesse?" She couldn't keep her voice from quavering as he deliberately ignored her. "What papers?"

The sudden slamming of the door behind him was the only response she got.

Crossing the room on leaden legs, she reached for the envelope, though every instinct for self-preservation screamed at her to run the other way. Desiree Hawthorne-Rainwater didn't run from her problems. Her father had pounded that into her from the moment she had taken her first step.

She pulled out a thick sheaf of papers.

"Jesse Rainwater vs. Desiree Hawthorne-Rainwater. Petition for Divorce on the Grounds of Irreconcilable Differences."

Her legs collapsed beneath her and she hit the ground, hard.

Divorce.

Irreconcilable differences.

Divorce.

Jesse wanted a divorce.

The papers slipped from her nerveless fingers as the words chased themselves around in her head.

Her husband—the father of her children—wanted a divorce.

Her partner—the man she'd loved for thirty-three years—*wanted a divorce.*

And she hadn't even seen it coming.

Desiree studied the bedroom door, seeing once more the contemptuous look Jesse had thrown at her before slamming out—as if simply being in the same room with her might somehow contaminate him.

A sob escaped before she could stifle it.

God, she was such a fool.

Eleven words. That's all the time or interest he'd had to spare. After twenty-seven years of marriage and a friendship that dated back over thirty years, their relationship could now be reduced to eleven measly words. Fewer, really. *This isn't working anymore. Sign the papers.*

Her stomach revolted and she grabbed the wastebasket by the bed just in time to prevent herself from throwing up all over the white Berber carpet.

When the nausea finally abated, she collapsed—prone on the floor. Too weak to get up, too shocked to do anything but stare into space.

What should she do now? she wondered.

What could she do?

Did she sign the papers?

Or fight?

She was so tired of fighting—she'd been doing it for so many years and on so many fronts that she didn't know if she had any fight left in her. Didn't know if what little she did have left was enough or if she had lost the war before the first battle was ever decided.

She tried to ignore her suddenly throbbing head, tried to plan a course of action. She was good at plans, she reminded herself—good at listing goals and plotting how to get there. She would just…

Just what? Desiree tried to think, to focus, but her mind refused to work. It's usual agility no match for the shock rocketing through her. She lifted a hand to press against her eyes, then stopped in midmotion, horrified to see it tremble. Her father would never have approved.

But what did she expect? She had been woefully, embarrassingly unprepared for this, completely blindsided by the idea of not having Jesse in her life. Of not being a part of his. Because no matter how bad things had gotten in the past few years, divorce had never been an option. She loved Jesse wholeheartedly and, until five minutes ago, would have sworn he felt the same.

Not anymore. Her fists clenched involuntarily, her

expensive—and unfamiliar—French manicure digging grooves into her palms as doubt assailed her again. How could she have been so wrong?

Pushing herself into a sitting position, she concentrated on breathing, to combat the bile scalding the back of her throat. In, out. In, out. Her eyes fell, unwittingly, to the carpet Jesse had been dead set against, swearing white had no place on a Thoroughbred ranch. Maybe he'd been right, as it now boasted numerous stains.

Without thinking, she sought out the light amber stain near the nightstand where Jesse had dropped his drink the first time she'd worn the red push-up bra and thong Willow had insisted she buy on her fortieth birthday. The bloodstain near the balcony where their oldest son, Rio, had sliced his forehead open when he was seven. She smiled absently—he'd been so brave. The red lipstick near the bathroom door—she'd dropped it years ago, when her youngest son, Dakota, had flown into the room and grabbed her around the waist, so thrilled at being named first-string varsity quarterback that he could barely get the words out.

The memories of a lifetime. Their lifetime.

Desiree tightly hugged her knees to her chest. She was cold all the way to the bone, despite the perfection of the late-December day. Willow had been afraid to hold the wedding outside, terrified that the capricious central Texas weather would ruin one of the most important days of her life. But Desiree had pushed for a garden wedding as images of the ranch decked out in sunshine and poinsettias danced through her mind. And she'd been right to push—the morning had dawned clear and bright. A perfect day to give her youngest child away.

She'd looked forward to this day for months, had even thought past the excitement of the wedding to how things would be when it was all over. When she and Jesse could snuggle on the couch and talk, finally, about this thing that had grown between them. About the plans she'd made to fix things.

What a joke she was.

Desiree swiped impatiently at her wet cheeks, disgusted with the tears that continued to fall. She could count on one hand the number of times she'd cried in the past thirty years, but her stoicism had deserted her completely.

What kind of woman was totally blindsided when her husband asked for a divorce? How could she not have known—she, who prided herself on knowing everything that happened on the ranch? How could she notice a stable boy's discontent and not see her own husband's misery? Was she really that blind?

Damn it, why hadn't he said something, anything, to clue her in to the fact that things had gotten so bad that divorce was the only option? When had he decided? Divorce papers weren't drawn up overnight—no matter how rich you were. How long had he known? How many days had he sat across from her at breakfast and known that he didn't love her anymore? How many nights had he worked beside her in the study knowing that he was leaving?

Yes, she'd recognized that things were going downhill between Jesse and her, just as she'd recognized that she was mostly to blame. But she'd thought she had all the time in the world to fix it, had put it off until a more convenient time. Until the kids were on their own. Until the ranch didn't need her so much.

Until Jesse no longer needed her at all. She really was her father's daughter after all.

JESSE TOOK THE STAIRS three at a time, desperate to get some fresh air. He was nauseous, his gut churning sickly as he realized he'd taken the last, irrevocable step necessary to end the relationship that had shaped most of his adult life. To sever all ties between himself and the love of his life. And he'd done it right before Christmas, on their daughter's wedding day. Could he have picked a worse day?

Slamming the front door behind him, he sucked huge gulps of air into his suddenly starving lungs. He closed his eyes, only to open them again as he saw Desiree's stricken face dancing on the back of his closed eyelids. Guilt ate at him making him even angrier because she was so clearly the one in the wrong.

He hadn't planned on doing it today, had had no intention of hurting Desiree on what should have been one of the happiest days of her life.

He'd been holding on to those papers for almost three weeks now—asking himself if he really wanted to go through with it. Telling himself he'd talk to her after the wedding, after Christmas, when things had settled down and they could discuss—rationally—what they should do about their pathetic excuse for a marriage.

But when he'd found out about the new trainer—*about his replacement, for God's sake*—he'd stopped thinking altogether. Fury had taken over, and it had been all he could do to keep from finding Mike and stuffing that damn article down his shrewd yet well-intentioned throat.

Jesse's hand slipped into his pocket of its own accord and he was staring at the fragment of newspaper before he realized what he was doing. As his eyes skimmed over the headline—again—he found himself thinking back on his conversation earlier that morning with Mike.

"Jesse Rainwater. You're just the man I've been wanting to see."

Startled by the unfamiliar voice booming from his living room, Jesse spilled some of the water he'd been pouring into the base of the eight-foot Christmas tree as he turned to investigate. A large sandy-haired man wearing a hat and suit was walking toward him, right hand extended.

"Mike?" he asked, eyebrows raised as he recognized the famous Thoroughbred rancher from Kentucky. "What are you doing here?" He put the watering can on a nearby table and headed toward the living room, grasping the man's outstretched hand in his own.

"I'm in town for the ceremony, of course. I couldn't miss my only nephew's wedding, could I?"

Jesse grinned. "Right. How did I manage to forget you were James's uncle?"

"Probably cuz things have been so crazy I wasn't able to make the engagement party or much of anything else."

"That would do it. I'm not sure if James is even here yet, but—"

"No, the boy's still at the hotel with his folks. I came early because I wanted to talk to you."

"Really? Well, have a seat." He gestured to the bar. "Can I get you something?"

"Much obliged—whiskey, straight up." Mike sat on the couch, stretching his long booted feet out in front of him. "I'm sure you're busy today, so I won't take up much of your time."

"All right." Jesse hoped he'd make it quick. He had a number of things he needed to get done—including checking on a couple of the horses and making sure the garden was properly set up before he changed for the ceremony.

"I've been watching you for a while, Jesse. Well, me and the rest of the horseracing community, that is."

"I've been watching you, too," Jesse answered. "That's part of the game, isn't it?"

"It is at that. But I've taken a personal interest in you, particularly with what's been going on with Cherokee's Dream and Born Lucky."

Stiffening at the mention of two of his own line of horses—a line that had been bred and trained away from the Triple H—Jesse stared at Mike through narrowed eyes. "They're not for sale."

Mike snorted, a broad grin on his tough, sun-wrinkled face. "I didn't expect they would be. I don't want to buy either of those horses."

"Then what do you want?"

"I want you to come and work with me."

Jesse laughed. "Yeah, right. Like that's going to happen."

"I'm serious. I want—"

"Look, Mike, I'm not looking for new employ-ment. And if I was, my wife would have something to say about me going to work for a major competitor."

"I bet she would at that." Mike took his hat off, tapped it against his thigh. "But I don't want you to work for me. I want to make you a partner."

"A partner? In what?"

"In my ranch, man. In Whistling Winds."

Thousands of thoughts whirled in Jesse's head as he stared at the man sitting across from him, but none of them made any sense. "You want to partner with the Triple H? I'll be honest—you need to be talking to Desiree. I don't think she'll go for it, but this is her ranch—"

"I didn't say anything about partnering with Desiree or the Triple H. I said I wanted to make *you* a partner in the ranch."

"Me?" Jesse ran a hand through his hair, totally bewildered by the completely unexpected offer. "Do you need money, Mike?"

Mike's laugh boomed out and he reached forward to slap Jesse on the back. "Not at all, man. Not at all."

"Then I don't understand what you're getting at. Why come all the way here and offer a partnership in your ranch? You've always guarded that ranch like a jealous fishwife."

"I still do. Much, I think, as Desiree guards this one." He leaned forward, took a sip of his drink. "Am I right?"

He was exactly right, but Jesse wouldn't admit it. He might be unhappy with the state of affairs on the ranch—and in his marriage—but he wasn't going to broadcast it. "That's pretty much the nature of the beast."

Mike nodded, apparently satisfied at his response. "Exactly."

"So, that still leaves me in the dark as to why you want to offer me part of your ranch."

"Not just part, Jesse. I'm willing to offer you one-third of Whistling Winds, turned over to you as soon as you sign the papers."

"One-third? What the hell do you want from me in return? My firstborn?"

"Hell, no." Mike laughed again. "I've got four kids of my own—I don't have room for any more. I want you to bring that small stable of horses you've developed away from here to breed and train on my ranch. I want those horses, and any others that you breed, buy or train, to run for the W."

"That's not going to happen."

"Why not?"

"My work is here. My life is here. I'm married to Desiree and I've been head trainer on the Triple H for over thirty years."

"What have you got to show for it?"

He bristled before he could stop himself. "What does that mean?"

"You know exactly what I mean. Everyone knows Desiree holds the strings on this ranch so tight that you'll never get a piece of it, whether you're her husband or not." He lifted a hand as though to forestall the explosion Jesse felt rising within him. "I can see I've touched a sore spot and that wasn't my intention. Nor am I insulting Desiree. She's done a hell of a job with this ranch since Big John died. No one can deny that or help being impressed by it.

"But at the same time, we both know this ranch wouldn't be where it is today if it didn't have you."

"Mike—"

"I'm getting old, we both are, and neither of us have time to sit around and blow smoke up each other's asses. You're the best trainer in North America, probably in the whole damn world. You've got the best eye for horseflesh I've ever seen and I need that eye, those skills, for my ranch.

"I've got the second-best Thoroughbred ranch in North America—you know it and so do I. I also know that the Triple H is better, and that's because of you. I don't want to get between you and your wife, and I'm not asking you to choose. I don't want you to come to my ranch and train my horses."

"You want me to come to your ranch and train *my* horses?" Jesse couldn't keep the incredulity from his voice.

"Exactly." Mike slapped his hat on his knee again. "And when they win—which we both know they will do—the credit goes to your brand. And mine."

"Of course. I get one-third of your ranch and you get—"

"The rights to half of your brand. We both know

that in three to five years Cherokee Dreaming will be *the* premier name on the racing circuit. And I have to assume Desiree knows it, too. Yet she hasn't made you a partner, has barely acknowledged that your stable exists."

"Mike—"

"I don't mean any disrespect to your wife, Jesse. God knows I'm not stupid enough to think that's the way to get you to agree with me. What I'm asking is if you want to be a part of something great. Not just work for a great ranch, but be part owner of one. You'll have the same freedom with your line that you've always had, but you'll have one hell of a financial backing behind you. You won't have to stable the line away from the ranch, won't have to fit in its development in your spare time. It'd be your only focus, your only responsibility and you'd get one-third of the profits brought in to my ranch by any of my horses."

Mike leaned forward, took a long swallow of his drink. "You'd be a fool to say no."

Jesse stood, walked slowly to the front window that looked out over the Triple H. This ranch had been his home for the past thirty-three years. Truth be told, *Desiree* had been his home all these long years. He'd decided weeks ago that he needed to find a new home, when he'd finally figured out that he couldn't be what Desiree wanted anymore.

He'd made his own plans, had expected to buy an acre or two of land somewhere and train his horses. He'd anticipated staying in Texas because he wanted to be close to his kids. But he'd never imagined an offer like this, had never dreamed of becoming a full partner in a ranch with the stature of Whistling Winds.

How could he have expected a relative stranger to make an offer like this when his own wife had never even considered offering him half as much? He turned, regarding Mike Jacoby through narrowed eyes.

He'd always respected him, had often been impressed with how he ran his ranch. "Still, we both know I'd be a fool to do anything right now."

Mike smiled as he settled his hat back on his head. "You're right. It's a big day for you and Desiree." He reached for the pocket on the inside of his suit jacket, pulling out a group of folded papers. "Here's the contract I've had drawn up. Look it over, let your lawyer look at it, whatever. Make notes on what you want changed and we'll negotiate."

"Look, Mike, I really don't think this is going to work."

"Well, I do. So take your time, think it over. A lot of the stuff in there is negotiable."

Jesse eyed the other man curiously. "What makes you so sure I'm going to go along with this? I am married to one of your biggest competitors, after all."

Mike stared at him for a long time, all sense of

levity gone from him. Finally, just when Jesse thought he wouldn't answer, he reached into his jacket and pulled out a folded up newspaper. "This ran a few weeks ago in the *Louisville Courier-Journal*. It made me think that now might be the time to put my plans into action." Dropping the newspaper article on the glass coffee table, he tapped a broad index finger on it a few times before rising to leave.

He stopped at the door. "If I'm wrong, then I apologize for bothering you. But the fact that you've listened this long makes me think I'm not wrong." He paused, then with a heavy sigh said, "I'm not screwin' with you, Jesse. Thirty-three percent of my ranch and the freedom to breed and train your horses any way you want. Give it some thought."

Jesse watched him slip out the front door, and though he knew that he needed to get going, he picked up the article Jacoby had left. Even knowing that he wouldn't like what it had to say couldn't prevent him from skimming the words.

Desiree Hawthorne-Rainwater, sole owner of the Triple H Thoroughbred Ranch, has long been revered in horse-racing circles for her knowledge and dedication to producing some of the best racehorses in the country and perhaps the world. Hawthorne-Rainwater has often attributed her success to her husband and head trainer, Jesse Rainwater, who she claims is "The best Thoroughbred trainer working in the world today." Yet, despite these claims, Hawthorne-Rainwater has recently, and discreetly, signed trainer Tom Bradford to replace Hawthorne as the Triple H's head trainer as early as January.

Rainwater has been at the Triple H for thirty-three years, having been hired by horse-racing legend Big John Hawthorne to revolutionize the historic Thoroughbred ranch's breeding and training programs. During his tenure, Rainwater has never had a year when one of the three-year-olds he's trained failed to win at least one of the races in the Triple Crown of horseracing—the Kentucky Derby, the Preakness and the Belmont Stakes. Many years, including this past one, his horses have won two of the races.

But a source close to Hawthorne-Rainwater cites her frustration at never having won all three races in one year—and therefore capturing the much-sought-after Triple Crown—as the number-one reason she has chosen to replace her husband after so many years. "Desiree has spent an incredible amount of time, money and effort to make sure she has the best ranch in the business. Her husband's failure to produce a horse capable of capturing the Triple Crown has become a frustration for her in recent years, one that she is no longer content to sit by and accept as inevitable. She believes Tom Bradford can bring the missing ingredient to the Triple H's training program and hopefully guarantee the ranch its first Triple Crown winner in over forty years."

Many in the horseracing community are surprised and unimpressed with Hawthorne-Rainwater's choice. "Jesse is the best trainer I've ever seen," says Baron Richardson, owner of the Bar L Thoroughbred Ranch of Louisville, Kentucky. "He has a natural affinity for horses that is rare, even in these circles. Tom Bradford is a good man and a great trainer, but he's not in Rainwater's class."

Bradford, who is currently employed by the Bells-and-Whistles Ranch of Atlanta, has produced numerous award-winning racehorses in the course of his career, including Jacy's Fancy, Hell's Bells and Whistling Dixie. Whistling Dixie, who has won over thirty races in her career, is best known for winning the Belmont Stakes in 2001.

Rainwater, who has trained such impressive horses as Crown's Majesty, Crown's Rhapsody and Royal Jewel, has recently started his own

stable of horses—Cherokee Dreaming—a
venture that many believe is partially responsible for Hawthorne-Rainwater's change of
heart. The horses of Dreaming Cherokee—
trained by Rainwater and his oldest son, Rio—
have already made a strong impression in the
American horseracing community.

Now, HOURS LATER THE agony still nearly brought
him to his knees.

How could Desiree have done this to him? To
them? How could she have gone behind his back and
hired someone to *replace* him without even giving
him a heads-up?

He shook his head. But then again, why was he
surprised? Desiree had always run this ranch how
she wanted and to hell with what he or anyone else
had to say.

His hand clenched involuntarily, crumpling the
paper into a ball before he could think better of it. Part
of him wanted to keep the article so that he could hurl
it at her later when the inevitable confrontation came.
But that was a childish desire, one he knew he wouldn't
give in to—no matter how angry she made him.

Besides, what was the use? The damage was done,
and he didn't think he'd ever be able to forgive her
her duplicity.

With a sigh Jesse tossed the crumpled article at the

nearest trash can—one of at least forty Desiree had had placed around the grounds for the upcoming ceremony and reception. Though he wanted nothing more than to sit in his study and brood, there was work to be done. His time at the Triple H was clearly coming to an end, but for now the horses were still his responsibility. He wouldn't let *them* down.

As he headed away from the house, he couldn't stop himself from turning and staring up at their bedroom window. Had she signed the papers? What would he do if she refused?

What would he do if she didn't?

CHAPTER TWO

DESIREE GAVE HERSELF A few more minutes to cry, but she was a Hawthorne through and through—her father had drilled the pride and responsibility of the name into her from an early age. In a little more than seven hours, three hundred people would be here, expecting the wedding of the year. She'd be damned if she'd greet them with puffy eyes.

She took a moment to get herself together. Though the wedding had been planned in meticulous detail—Willow really had missed her calling as an army general—there were a few small tasks that still needed to be done. She had to get out of this room, keep moving, hold things together for another twelve hours or so.

Climbing to her feet, she crossed the room, then threw open the balcony doors and let the cool air flow over her as she surveyed the ranch that had been in her family for generations. This land was hers—as far as the eye could see and beyond. Passed from her great-grandfather to her grandfather to her father to her. The first woman to inherit in four generations. Had she worked so hard to be worthy of the name that she'd neglected the only man she'd ever loved? Had she somehow let what she felt for the ranch negate what she felt for Jesse?

She pushed the questions to the back of her mind, knowing that she'd have to deal with them eventually. Just not today. She fought to focus on the details to be attended to instead of the headache behind her eyes. She still had to check on the caterer, talk with the florist, make sure the ballroom was in order for the reception. But first she needed to get a couple of things.

Something borrowed.

She crossed to her jewelry box, pulled out the string of pearls she'd worn to her own wedding, just as her mother had done before her. Willow, so enthralled with the past that she had made plans to wear them almost as soon as she'd told James yes, had picked her gown because it looked best with the necklace.

Desiree could only hope they would bring her daughter more luck then they'd obviously brought her. Slipping the pearls into her pocket, she made a wish for her daughter's happiness. Wished that Willow would never feel the rage and fear that pounded through her mother at this very moment.

Something blue.

Turning slightly, she stared at the bookcase near

the door that held the many volumes that chronicled her life. Big John had been a huge stickler for details and an even bigger one for recording history. From childhood he'd drilled into her the importance of her place on the ranch, and from there, her place in history. It had become second nature to spend a few minutes every couple of days recording the events of her daily life in all their glory and monotony.

She'd promised Willow that her something blue could be her first journal—the one that told the story of Jesse's and her relationship. As a teenager Willow had pored over the book, and Desiree had known, even before Willow ever gave voice to it, that she'd wanted to be swept off her feet as her mother had been so many years before. It had finally happened—later than it had for Desiree—but Willow had gotten her heart's desire.

Desiree steeled herself as she reached for the lapis-blue journal Jesse had given her years before, told herself it was just a book. Still, her hand shook as she grasped the journal, and though she was determined not to open it, in the end she couldn't help herself.

She turned the cover with trembling hands, read the dedication Jesse had written on the inside of the front cover. But before she could work up the nerve to read the first entry, a knock sounded and her daughter's voice carried through the heavy wood door.

"Mom?"

Desiree opened her mouth to speak, but all that came out was a low-pitched croak. Clearing her throat, she took a deep breath and tried again. "Come on in, honey."

Willow entered, looking so beautiful it nearly broke her heart. She was still dressed in her robe, her hair and makeup not yet done for the wedding. But she was tall and elegant, her nails done to perfection and her brown eyes so full of hope.

Had Desiree looked like that once? Had the mere thought of Jesse brought a similar glow to her face? Of course it had—from the moment she'd first laid eyes on him until…

Until when? When had the glow faded? When had the small irritations of daily life worn away the joy and passion, the hope and anticipation, until all that was left was pain? And love—even as the glow of youth faded, her love for Jesse had endured. It had endured more than three decades, would have endured at least three more, if he hadn't done this. If he hadn't…

"Mom, are you okay?"

Desiree jerked. "I'm fine, baby." She reached out a hand, ran it softly down Willow's cheek. "Just thinking about how things are changing."

"I love you, Mama."

"I love you, too, sweetheart," Desiree answered as Willow threw her arms around her. The fuzziness that had clutched at her since Jesse had tossed down the divorce papers finally cleared as the strain in her daughter's voice registered.

Desiree pulled back, stared into her daughter's eyes. "What's going on, Will?"

"I'm just happy." Willow raised an unsteady hand to wipe at her eyes, but her smile trembled at the corners.

Eyebrows lifted, Desiree stared at her youngest child. "That's a pretty pathetic smile for someone who's crying from joy."

"Mama, don't." The request was almost a wail as Willow pulled away.

"Don't be concerned when my only daughter comes in here looking devastated on what should be the happiest day of her life?" Desiree grasped Willow's hands in her own.

"I'm scared," Willow blurted. "I'm really scared."

"Of course you are. That's perfectly normal—"

"No, it's not. Not like this." She turned away abruptly, strode to the balcony and stared out at the ranch.

Desiree sighed, ran a hand through her own short, disheveled crop of hair as she searched for the right words. Yesterday they would have been right there, waiting for her to speak them. But today…today only emptiness remained.

"What if I'm making a mistake?" Willow's voice

was soft and trembly, so unlike her youngest child that Desiree had a moment of alarm.

"Do you think you are?"

"I don't know! That's why I'm here, talking to you."

"Oh." Desiree nodded. "I see."

"What do you see? Tell me, Mama." Willow's movements were agitated. "I'm not like you—I've never been like you."

Desiree snorted. "Of course you aren't. Why should you be like anyone but yourself?

"Come sit with me, baby," she murmured when her daughter didn't answer, drawing Willow to the small love seat by the window. "Now what is this all about?"

Willow shrugged even as she buried her head against Desiree's neck. "How did you know, so fast, that Daddy was the right one for you?"

Desiree stiffened, stifling her own pain. She wrapped her arms around her youngest child and rocked her slowly, as she had done when Willow was a child.

"I just did, sweetie. One look at him and my heart recognized him as mine."

Willow shuddered. "It wasn't like that for me with James. It was slow, unexpected. It crept up on me and then suddenly, one day…"

"You knew you loved him."

"I guess." Willow took a deep breath, pulled slowly away. "One day I woke up and realized that I should spend the rest of my life with James. He's perfect for me—he calms me down, he listens to me, he—"

"Turns you on."

"Mama!"

"Willow!" Desiree echoed her daughter's shocked tone with some amusement. "Just because I'm almost fifty doesn't mean I'm dead. And it'd be a really bad idea to marry a man you're not attracted to."

"I know that. It's just—"

"Just what?"

"Shouldn't I be one hundred percent sure? Shouldn't I know, without a doubt, that this is what I want? You knew you wanted Daddy, you knew you could never be happy with anyone else. I just want that same kind of certainty."

Desiree fought the little voice inside of her that wanted to yell, "And look where that's gotten me!"

Biting back the bitter words, Desiree turned to stare directly into the troubled darkness of her daughter's eyes. "Life isn't always certain, Willow. You make the best decision for you based on what you think and feel at the time. You can't tell the future and you can't live your life second-guessing yourself."

"But you—"

"Stop it." The words came out harsher than she'd intended, and Willow jerked back in surprise. Desiree sighed, reached up to smooth her daughter's hair. "You're not me. You're not living my life. It's absurd to expect things to play out exactly the same way."

"I just want to be as certain as you were, as certain as Daddy was."

This time she couldn't stop the harsh laugh from exploding out of her. "Your father was nowhere near as sure as I was. Not by a long shot."

"What do you mean? Your journals—"

"My journals are written from my point of view. Not your dad's." She stood and walked out onto the balcony, watching as the florist's van drove up and Maria, their longtime housekeeper, went out to greet it.

"Willow, your father was very unsure about marrying me. Between the age difference and the money difference and your grandfather, he was certain he was making a mistake." She turned to look at her daughter's shocked face and this time her smile was genuine. "He figured we wouldn't last six months, thought I'd cave to my father's demands and the whispers of people around us."

Willow's eyes were wide, shocked. "But he married you anyway? Why?"

Like Desiree hadn't asked herself that question at least a thousand times in the past hour? How could she answer her daughter's question when she didn't have a clue herself? She debated her options. Finally, opting for the truth, she said, "I don't know."

"Mama—"

"What are you so afraid of?

"What if this is all just a huge mistake I'll grow to regret? You and Dad—"

"What about your father and me?"

"You started out so happy, so in love. And then…" Willow's voice trailed off uncomfortably.

Desiree grimaced. Had their problems in recent years really been so obvious? If Willow knew, did that mean that Rio and Dakota did as well? The thought flattened her, devastating her when she thought she couldn't get any more distraught. She searched for something to say to reassure her daughter.

"Honey, no one knows the future. No one knows at the beginning of a marriage how or when the end will come. Through death fifty years later or divorce in five years, nothing is guaranteed."

"That's my point. Why should I take this risk when it could end badly?"

Desiree shook her head, astounded at how good her daughter was at complicating things. How could she have forgotten that sympathy and understanding never got her anywhere with Willow? Just as she'd forgotten that Willow was more than capable of calling the wedding off because of a few last minute doubts.

"What if it doesn't?" She hadn't forgotten how to snap her daughter out of a good old-fashioned pity party.

"That's the best you've got?" Willow's voice was incredulous. "You've got to be kidding me."

"I've already told you everything I know about the subject. What else do you want me to say?"

"I want you to say that I'm *not* making a mistake, that James is a great guy, that I love him and he loves me."

"You already know all that, don't you?"

"Yes, but what if that's not enough?"

Willow's words slammed through her like a freight train. When had life gotten so mixed up that love ceased to be enough?

Had it ever been enough? Or had she just been stupid to think that it was?

She stared at her daughter, the silence in the room thickening. When she finally spoke, her voice was harsher than she'd intended. "What do you want, Willow Rose? A money-back guarantee that nothing bad's going to happen to you? An iron-clad agreement that this is going to work out exactly like you planned?"

"Mom—"

"Because life doesn't work like that. Everything isn't always right or wrong, black or white. Sometimes it's shades of gray. Sometimes—" She broke off at Willow's shocked expression, bit back the words that burned in her throat, in her gut. She crossed the room to rest her palm on her daughter's cheek.

"I'm sorry, baby."

"It's okay." But the words were jerky and her daughter rigid beneath her hands.

"No, it's not." Her hand slipped down to Willow's chin and she gently tipped her face up until they were eye-to-eye. "Do you love him?"

"Yes, but—"

"No buts. Do you love him?"

"Yes."

"Does James love you?"

"Yes."

"Do you want to build a life with him?"

"Yes."

"Have children with him?"

"Of course." Willow's eyes were huge, but the smile that trembled on her lips was suddenly real again.

"Grow old with him?"

"Eventually."

"Then what else are you looking for, Willow?" Desiree smoothed a hand over her daughter's long, black hair, stared into her heavily lashed, almond-shaped eyes. Jesse's hair, Jesse's eyes. Nausea churned, but she steadfastly beat it back.

"Today's about a promise. Forget everything else. Forget the dresses, the people watching, all the planning. It's all superfluous. Today is about a promise—the promise you'll make to James and the one he'll make to you."

She stared out at the green and endless land she'd sacrificed everything for. "Have you ever broken a promise to James before?"

"Never."

"Has he ever broken one to you?"

"Of course not."

Desiree looked her daughter straight in the eye, even as anguish burned through her. "Then what else is there? If you trust him not to break his promises, if you know that you won't break yours, what is there to be afraid of? Today he'll promise to love and honor you forever and you'll do the same for him."

"Forever's a long time, Mama."

Desiree's smile was bittersweet. "It's only as long as you want it to be, baby. How long is that?"

Willow's eyes grew soft and faraway, and Desiree could all but see the future in them. "An eternity, at least." She smiled. "Thanks, Mama."

Desiree winked. "Don't mention it. What good would I be if my kids couldn't ask for advice every now and again? Anything else?"

"No, I think you've covered it." Willow rushed into her embrace, and Desiree savored the feel of her little girl in her arms, savored the rush of love and warmth.

A knock sounded at the door. "Willow?" called Anna softly. She was Willow's oldest friend and her maid of honor. "Felipe is here to do your hair."

"I'm coming," Willow called, rushing toward the door. "Thanks, Mom."

"That's what I'm here for. Oh, hey, don't forget the necklace and journal." She gestured to the items on the dresser.

"I'll get them later—I'm so scatterbrained today I'll probably lose them if I take them now."

"Have fun with the girls," Desiree commented, smiling at Willow's renewed enthusiasm. She kept smiling even as she remembered the promises Jesse had made to her through the years. Promises she'd counted on. Promises she'd never thought he'd break.

Her eyes fell, again, on the journal gleaming bright blue in the sunlight that poured through the open doors. She picked it up, to put it back on the shelf so it wouldn't get misplaced. But her hands paged through it of their own volition, searching, seeking that first…

And then she found it. Her fingers reached out, traced the letters on the page and her heart broke at the love revealed in every word. She really was a bigger fool than she thought.

CHAPTER THREE

When I woke that morning, it seemed like any other morning on the ranch. It was spring, so the fields were alive with color, animal babies wandered the meadows and life was good. I was sixteen and it was hard to imagine life as anything but wonderful.

I was trained at an early age to believe that the Triple H was everything. It was worth any amount of money, any personal sacrifice, any human life. Preserving it was my father's destiny, and through him, my destiny as well. I had believed this all sixteen years of my life—had eaten, breathed, dreamed the ranch as the only child of Big John was supposed to. I had never given that destiny much thought, though it was always there, somewhere, in the back of my mind.

At least it always had been, until that first Thursday in April.

I had been out riding, as I did every morning

before school. It was early, maybe 6:00 a.m., but light had streaked the sky for nearly an hour. I reigned Jezebel in hard, both of us exhilarated from the high-spirited romp we had just finished around the outskirts of the ranch. She and I loved going there because it was different than the other parts of the Triple H—wilder, more natural, closer to the earth and to God.

I was washing Jezzie down, walking her around the paddock and plying her with sugar cubes from my pocket. My father's voice, booming like a Texas thunderstorm, carried from the house to the paddock and caught my attention. He was laughing as he walked toward me, talking to a man I didn't recognize.

I stared at the two of them, unable to look away. My heart started pounding, my breath grew shallow and I learned, in only a moment, what destiny truly was.

"DESI, SWEETIE, COME meet our new head trainer," Big John called to her across three corrals.

Head trainer? The words whirled around in her head as she struggled for breath. This man was the new trainer? The one Daddy had been running after for nearly a year? The one who, at thirty-one, had trained more winning Thoroughbreds than most trainers did in their entire careers?

Her father called to her again and she headed toward him, swinging the gate shut on the paddock as she went. How could her father not see it? She might only be sixteen years old, but even she could recognize the combination of power and danger that oozed from this man's every pore.

"Jesse, I'd like you to meet my daughter, Desiree. Desi, this is Jesse Rainwater. He's only thirty-one and already the best trainer in this hemisphere, and he's agreed to work here. He's going to bring us our next Triple Crown winner."

"Hello, Desiree. Nice to meet you."

The smooth silk of his voice sent shivers up and down her spine as she stared at him, tongue-tied. He was tall and dark, with eyes that looked right through her. Desiree had never paid much attention to the male of the species, but Jesse was impossible to ignore. More than a decade too old for her, he did without trying what all of the high school boys had failed to do. He curled her toes with just a look.

From his too-long black hair to his black-magic eyes, everything about him appealed to her. His Levi's were faded to white in places and his black T-shirt molded every muscle he had—muscles that had obviously come from hard work and not those toys at the gym. The hand that grasped her outstretched one was rough and callused, and numerous scars stood out against the deep bronze of his skin.

Nothing about Jesse escaped Desiree's notice and she could tell that nothing about the Triple H escaped his.

He seemed to note every trainer and assistant, every workout boy and groom. Whatever his past, whatever his circumstances, in those moments he looked around the ranch as if he had finally found a home.

Desiree cleared her suddenly thick throat, found her voice. "Good to meet you, Mr. Rainwater."

He smiled, a brief curve of those finely chiseled lips, and her heart beat double time. "Call me Jesse."

Taking a few deep breaths, she focused her eyes slightly over his left shoulder, hoping her father wouldn't comment on her odd reaction. "Okay…Jesse." Desi's voice was breathless, shaky, and she cleared her throat again, praying no one had noticed.

Big John's eyes narrowed on her face. "Are you getting sick again?" He turned to Jesse. "Desi's getting over a bout with pneumonia—kept her laid up for two weeks."

Her face burned while anxiety cramped her stomach. "I'm fine, Daddy. Just something in my throat." If her father thought for one second that she was sick, she'd be stuck in the house for another two weeks. Big John took no chances with his only child.

"She looks fine to me," Jesse interceded, as if he could read her thoughts.

Desiree's eyes went gratefully to his and she flushed even more at his discreet wink. "I am fine, Daddy. Honest."

"All right, then. You want to help me show Jesse the ranch?"

"Can I? Really?" She loved showing off the Triple H and Big John knew it.

"Yes, really." He laughed, patted her shoulder. "Let's go."

"I can't yet. I have to finish taking care of Jezebel." She gestured to the horse her parents had given her on her fourteenth birthday.

"We'll wait." Jesse was the one who spoke.

Her eyes darted to her father for approval and he shrugged good-naturedly. "Sure we will. You need some help, sweetheart?"

"I've got it, Daddy. It'll only take a couple of minutes." Hands shaking, heart in her throat, Desi was conscious of Jesse watching her intently, even as he spoke to her father about the horses. Despite the nearly overwhelming desire to rush, she rubbed Jezebel down and brushed her thoroughly. The horse shouldn't have to suffer just because her owner had suddenly lost her mind.

Even in the early morning the Texas sun was strong, and she was uncomfortably aware of how she looked. Sweat molded her faded T-shirt to her back, and her comfy old jeans had so many holes in them Mama constantly threatened to throw them out. Her unwashed red hair was scraped into a ponytail, and a zit was blooming on her chin. She could ride a horse like nobody's business and could quote more racing statistics than most professional gamblers, but she knew she'd never win any beauty contests.

Finally, *finally,* Jezebel was groomed and the three of them set out to walk the ranch. As her father and Jesse talked about racing, she hung back a little and watched him. Like the other trainers they had had on the ranch, Jesse talked to the horses soothingly as he looked them over. But there was something different about how he did it. Looking into the horses' eyes, softly stroking their necks, Desi could see him form a connection with them.

She glanced at her dad, saw him watching Jesse with a speculative look in his eyes. Maybe it was his Native American heritage, maybe it was just a natural affinity for horses, but it sure looked as though he was reading those horses' minds and they were reading his.

Leaving the smaller stables, which housed some of the retired horses and their very young offspring, they headed for the first of the five huge racing stables. They had almost reached the door when a commotion broke out in a paddock behind them.

She turned to look and felt the color drain from her face as she started to run. Crown's Majesty, the best two-year-old stallion the Triple H had and the current hope for next year's Triple Crown, was spooked. He'd gotten away from his handler and was out of control. He knocked George down and reared up on his hind legs, preparing to come down hard on the unfortunate exercise boy.

As she ran toward the horse, Desi was conscious of her father and Jesse running next to her. "Get out of the way," her dad shouted, as George rolled away from the razor sharp hooves.

She ran faster, heart pounding. Fear was a living, breathing thing inside of her. The situation was critical and she knew it. Stallions were notoriously high-strung, and Majesty was the highest strung of them all. She feared for George but she also feared for the horse. In a rage like this, Majesty could injure himself and never feel it until later. And by then his chances of ever racing again could be over.

Jesse poured on the speed, running past Desiree and her father as if they weren't even there. He was staring intently at the horse, and she knew he too realized how potentially dangerous the situation was. He stopped running about fifteen feet from Majesty and began talking to the frightened horse.

Her breath caught in her throat. She knew Jesse was the best at what he did—her dad had been talking about him nonstop for months—but he didn't know Majesty and the horse certainly didn't know him.

Big John, thinking along the same lines as her, moved to intercede, but stopped at Jesse's abrupt hand motion.

The sounds Jesse crooned made no sense. Not words, just a musical collection of sounds running together. Desiree held her breath as Majesty snorted angrily, turning toward Jesse as if to eliminate this new threat.

She swallowed a scream as the horse charged. She expected Jesse to jump out of the way, but he didn't. He held his ground, facing down the charging horse. Just when she was sure that he'd be trampled to death, he took one step to the side. As the rampaging horse ran past him, he grabbed Majesty's mane and swung lightly into the saddle, still crooning soothingly.

Desiree and Big John stared, openmouthed, as Majesty twisted and turned, trying to dislodge Jesse. But even they could tell that it was a halfhearted rebellion. Within sixty seconds he'd given up the attempt to knock Jesse off his back, and instead allowed Jesse to guide him into a gentle walk.

As breath slowly returned to her tortured lungs, Desi became aware again of her surroundings. Everyone within visual distance of the altercation had stopped. Grooms and trainers alike stared at Jesse with respect. She, too, stood in absolute awe at what he had done with a horse he'd never met before.

And Majesty wasn't just any horse; he was the nastiest, most hot-tempered horse the Triple H had ever bred. Yet he'd responded to Jesse like a sweet-tempered colt out for an afternoon jog. It was truly inspiring to see.

Overriding the awe and respect Jesse had earned was an overwhelming curiosity, a need to know exactly how he'd done what he'd done and a desire to learn from him. So she stood quietly, as her father and other men rushed forward to congratulate Jesse. He was calm amidst all the commotion, ignoring the compliments and questions. He simply dismounted and began walking Majesty toward his stable. Desi tagged along behind, not willing to lose sight of him for an instant.

Once inside, Alan, the ranch's business manager, called to Big John. He excused himself for a minute, leaving Jesse and her alone with the horses.

She almost stayed silent, worried about embarrassing herself in front of the most beautiful man she'd ever seen. But curiosity got the best of her, as it so often did, and she asked, "What are you doing?"

He looked at her, his black eyes carefully blank. "What do you mean?"

"You're talking to that horse and he's talking to you." She watched his eyes go wide in surprise. "And not with your voice. I saw you do it with Majesty earlier."

He smiled wryly. "No one's ever noticed before."

She flushed. Probably because no one had ever studied him as intently as she was. "You look different when you do it. Your eyes go kind of hazy and it's like you're not here anymore."

He nodded. "I can walk with animals. That's what my grandfather called it. My mother, too."

She was fascinated. "So, you're Native American?"

He stiffened and his eyes grew a little wary. "I'm half Cherokee."

"That's awesome." She cleared her throat, nervous under his intense scrutiny. "How does it work?"

He paused for a minute, then smiled as if he understood her curiosity to know everything about him. "I don't know exactly. One person in each generation of my family has the gift. By the time I was six, everyone knew it was me. I don't know why I was chosen."

"Because you won't abuse it. You're strong and you hold your power well. But there's no cruelty in you." Her hands flew to her mouth almost before she was done speaking. Mama always told her to think before she spoke and she had gotten better at it. Except, it seemed, with Jesse. "I'm sorry. I didn't mean—"

"That's all right." He eyed her speculatively. "How do you know that?"

"I just do."

"That's not an answer." His black eyes pinned her in place, demanded an answer that she didn't want to give.

"You know things about animals? Things no one else does. Right?"

He nodded. "So what?"

"It's like that for me, with people. I just know things. Daddy says I've got good instincts. Mama says it's a curse to see so much about others."

"What do you think?"

"I don't, really. It's not something I think about. It's just there, you know?"

"I do, actually."

"I figured you might." She smiled at him shyly.

"How old are you?"

"Sixteen."

He nodded as his eyes swept around the stable and out to the land beyond the open door. "What's your favorite part of the ranch, Desiree?"

Shivers worked their way up and down her spine. No one ever called her by her full name, largely because she hated it. Something about being named after a long-dead great-grandmother had creeped her out from the time she was a little girl, but the way *he* said it—in that rough satin voice—made her appreciate her name for the first time. She shrugged again. "I don't know."

He cocked his head to the left, the look on his face patently disbelieving. "Yes, you do."

"The training circles." Desi blurted the truth without stopping to think.

"Why?" His intense concentration made her nervous. He studied her the way he studied the horses, as if he was examining every thought in her head.

"They're about becoming. No one's won, no one's lost. It's just pure potential. Just a horse and a dream, before reality intrudes."

His lips turned up slightly at the corners in the first smile she'd seen that reached his eyes. "So you're a romantic."

"Aren't all teenage girls?"

"I don't know. You're the first teenage girl I've talked to since I was a teenage boy."

She giggled. "Then you've got a lot to learn."

"I guess I do at that." Silence reigned for a few moments. Finally he said, "You know, my culture believes strongly in special gifts—strange, inexplicable talents that only a few people have."

"Obviously. Look at what you can do. People would have to be pretty cynical if they could still doubt that extra-sensory talents exist after witnessing your connection with that horse out there."

He turned until he was fully facing her. "I wasn't talking about me."

"Oh." She glanced away, blushing despite her best efforts not to. "Then—"

"You understand things you're too young to know about. You see things others can't."

"Yes."

"So can I ask you a question about that?"

"You mean you haven't already?"

He laughed. It sounded kind of rusty, as if he'd almost forgotten how. "I'm serious. What do you see when you look at me?"

Too much. She saw too much when she looked at him. She saw the surface—the handsomest, sexiest, most amazing man in the whole world. She saw the brilliant horse trainer, the one who walked in the minds of animals. She saw loneliness, the self-imposed isolation, though she didn't know why. And clearly, so clearly, she saw what he would be for the Triple H and for her. The future. *Her* future.

But she couldn't tell him any of that. Not this man whom she had just met. This man who was too old for her, too serious and too hard by far. So she said simply, "A guy who works for my father." It was lame, but she didn't know how else to answer.

She wasn't ready for him yet and he certainly wasn't ready for her.

DESI CAME BACK TO herself with a start, turning the pages of the journal as she skimmed through the next few months' worth of entries. There was nothing much of interest there—at least not for a soon-to-be-divorced woman of forty-nine.

After all, her response to his question had set the tone for the next eighteen months of their relationship. She had chased after him, wanting to spend every waking moment with him and he put up with it, though he never again opened himself up to her. Until one night, when everything between them changed with one random act of violence.

Out of habit, and a need she refused to admit even to herself, Desiree flipped to the seventh entry in the book, one she—and her daughter—knew by heart.

I was seventeen the first time Jesse ever touched me. I mean really touched me, not just a pat on the back or an affectionate ruffle of my hair. It was prom night and I was all dressed up—hot-pink halter dress, sky-scraper heels, a new haircut and more makeup on my face than I normally wore in a year. I was uncomfortable, miserable, con-vinced I would humiliate myself by losing my balance in the five-inch heels and tumbling onto my butt in front of my date and the entire senior class.

I hadn't wanted to go to the stupid dance, hadn't wanted to waste time I could spend with Jesse on a stupid high school boy. But Mama had insisted, had finally convinced me that I would regret missing this dance for the rest of my life. She even went so far as to line up my date for me—I think she was afraid I would buck tradition and go by myself. Fear that was, truthfully, well-grounded.

Mama was tenacious. Before I knew what was happening, I'd been whisked into her favorite salon for a facial, manicure, pedicure, haircut and some other tortures too painful to mention. She found the dress, bought the shoes, even presented me with my very first pair of diamond earrings on the day of the dance.

The evening started out ordinarily enough. Steven picked me up in his father's Cadillac, took me out to dinner then danced with me for hours once we arrived at prom. I tried to be enthusiastic, tried to enjoy the dancing and the festivities despite my awkward nervousness and aching feet. Steven was a gentleman— funny, attentive, interesting—and eventually I relaxed enough to enjoy the dance and the party he took me to afterward.

When we got back to the ranch sometime after three in the morning, I was happy, a little excited and too restless to sleep. So I took off my shoes and invited Steven, a city boy, to the stables to meet Jezebel. When he reached for my hand, I let him, because it had been a nice night and the gesture seemed harmless.

I introduced him to my horse, laughed as he fed Jezebel sugar cubes and cracked jokes at his own expense. When he wrapped an arm around me and lowered his head to mine, I didn't protest because I was curious. Obsessed with Jesse from the first moment I had laid eyes on him, I had missed out on the many dating rituals of my peers. I was seventeen and had never been kissed, had never been held by an attractive boy, had never felt the rush of desire as hands smoothed over my body.

His lips met mine and the sensation was mildly pleasant—not earth-shattering, not arousing, not even very interesting. I pulled back with a smile, said something funny, turned to leave. And just then suddenly he changed. He grabbed me, pulled me to him, his hands moving hard and fast over my arms, my back, my breasts. I tried to pull away, tried to shove him back, but he was strong and aroused and I had nowhere to go.

DESI SCREAMED AS Steven dragged her to the ground, his hand slipping inside her dress to fondle her bare breast even as he thrust his tongue deep into her mouth. She gagged and turned her head, her body bucking desperately beneath his.

"Stop it! Steven, I mean it. I want you to stop."

"You don't mean that." His breathing was harsh as he forced her legs apart, settling himself between her thighs and rubbing himself against her. "You can't."

"I do. I do. Steven, no!" Her voice was panicked, her hands shaking as she shoved against his face. Annoyance gave way to anger and anger to fear as time stood still and she realized that she couldn't move, that he had her pinned beneath him and that there was no one around to hear her screams.

She strained against him, her body inching along the ground as she fought to escape him. "Come on, Des, stop fighting." Steven's voice was low, but she could hear the strain in it as he struggled to keep her beneath him. "You'll like it. I promise."

Adrenaline surged through her and she put her hands on his forehead, pushing against him with every ounce of strength she possessed. His head snapped back, an almost comical look of surprise replacing the desire in his eyes. It only took a second for him to come to his senses, but that second was all Desi needed.

She rolled away from him and ran. Dirt and hay clung to her dress but she didn't notice as she raced for the door. He caught her mere seconds from freedom, his hands grabbing the hem of her dress and tugging so hard that she stumbled and the material ripped.

She kicked out as she fell, her foot catching him squarely in the chest. She heard the air rush from his lungs as her heel connected and she scrambled, on all fours, desperate to escape this nightmare that was spiraling completely out of her control.

Spying a shovel near the door, Desiree extended her body, reached for it, pausing only a second as she waited to feel her hand close around the wooden handle. But that moment of hesitation was all it took for him to be on her, one hand shoving her face into the ground as his other lifted her dress and ripped frantically at her pink lace underwear.

"No! Please, no!" The words were torn from her against her will, shrill cries that sounded nothing like her voice. She tried to move, her fingers clawing at the ground as she twisted against him. But he was on top of her and he outweighed her by at least sixty pounds.

Tears streamed down her face as strangled sobs tore through her chest. She wanted to scream, to beg, to plead, but he was too heavy and she couldn't breathe. She heard the rasp of his zipper, felt her dress tear again as the lack of air caught up to her and the world slowly turned gray around the edges.

"Steven, please." The words were hardly more than a whisper, the fight all but gone from her as she began to float silently away. Her lungs shuddered, desperate for air as tears leaked slowly down her chin to mingle with the dirt beneath her cheek.

She felt so heavy, as if she weighed a thousand pounds. Much too heavy to move or struggle. Desiree's eyes drifted slowly shut despite her determination to fight. She felt him push against her, heard a bellow of rage that didn't register.

She heard a scream from far away, followed by a crash and then, suddenly, she was free. Her lungs were on fire as she sucked in gulp after gulp of oxygen.

She could hear Steve whimpering behind her, could hear the slap of flesh hitting flesh. She struggled to her hands and knees and tried to get to her feet, but her legs felt like jelly.

"Stay there, Desiree. Don't move." Jesse's voice bit off the words, and relief pumped through her. They were only five words, but they were the five sweetest words she'd ever heard. Jesse was here. Everything would be okay. *She* would be okay.

Another crash, another groan. She turned in time to see a bruised and bloody Steven hit the wall face-first. "Are you okay?" It was Jesse's voice again, harsher than she'd ever heard it. She stared at him, watched his eyes burn with a rage so black it nearly frightened her.

"I'm fine, Jesse." Her voice was hoarse, raw. Jesse snarled at the sound, his eyes taking in her torn dress and mud-streaked face, her bruised flesh and shaking body.

With a growl of fury, he buried his fist in Steven's stomach. The power of the blow drove Steven to his knees and he knelt on the ground, retching. His clothes were now as torn and dirty as hers, his nose bled profusely and his arms were wrapped defensively around his stomach when Jesse reached down and grabbed him by the back of his shirt.

All but carrying him from the barn, Jesse stopped at the door and pinned Desiree with a look that demanded obedience. "Don't move until I get back. I need to check you for injuries."

Desiree watched Jesse propel Steven forward without breaking a sweat. She was still on her hands and knees and suddenly incredibly conscious of what she must look like. She pushed herself up, struggling to her feet. She tried to get to the door and see what Jesse would do to Steven, but her shaky legs refused to support her.

"I told you not to move," Jesse said as he entered the barn and crossed the space between them quickly. "I meant it."

"I'm fine," she said from between her chattering teeth.

"Shut up." His voice was low and tender as he crouched next to her, his hands running over her neck, down her arms and across her torso as he searched for injuries. "Did he—"

"No," she answered loudly, interrupting him before he could say the ugly word. "No," she repeated more softly as she looked into Jesse's concerned face.

"Are you sure?" He was looking at the torn skirt and the ripped bodice of her fancy dress.

Color stained her cheeks and she crossed her arms defensively over her bare breasts. "I'm fine, Jesse. You got here before—" Her voice broke. "You got here in time."

"I'm glad, darlin'." His voice was thick as he slipped off his blue T-shirt and helped her pull it over her head. "So damn glad."

"Me, too." She looked away, unable to bear the pity and kindness reflected in his eyes.

"Are you hurt? I didn't feel anything broken, but that doesn't mean—"

She shook her head as tears clogged her throat. She wanted to be anywhere but here, to be with anyone but him. Though Jesse's arms felt amazing and she could smell his scent from the T-shirt, she wished him far, far away. She was vulnerable, humiliated. She had wanted him for two years, had woven dreams around him. And the first time he'd seen her naked had been like this.

He grasped her chin with gentle fingers and turned her head until she was facing him. Desiree blinked rapidly, but there was no doubt he saw the tears, saw the embarrassment and the agony. "Let's get you home to your mother," he said, scooping her into his arms.

Despite the fear coursing through her and the aches in muscles she hadn't known existed, Desiree turned her head into his chest. After all the hours and days and years of dreaming, it felt almost unreal to be held in his arms. She reveled in it, pushing Steven and what he'd almost done to the back of her mind. Then Jesse's words registered and she began to squirm.

"No, Jesse! You can't!" She pulled back, stared into his concerned, confused face.

"Can't what?" he demanded as he stopped.

"Mama can't know about this."

"Of course she needs to know about this!" He scowled fiercely and his eyes narrowed with renewed rage.

"No, Jesse." She pushed against his chest until he set her onto her feet. "I mean it. I'm not telling Mama and you aren't, either."

"You think so?" When she didn't answer, simply crossed her arms over her chest and glared at him, he continued, "Desiree, be reasonable. You were attacked, would have been raped had I not come along when I did. Your parents need to know."

Biting her lip, Desi turned away, unable to bear the concern in Jesse's eyes, the softening he didn't try to hide.

"She picked him, Jesse."

"What?"

She shrugged. "Mama arranged my date with Steven. I didn't want to go to the stupid dance, but she insisted. She took care of everything—my dress, my hair—" she gestured helplessly toward the door "—my date. If I told her how things ended—almost ended—she'd be devastated.

"She doesn't need the guilt on top of everything else, Jesse."

He sighed, his hands clasping her shoulders gently. "Desi, she's your mother. Don't you think she'd want to know? Doesn't she have the right to know?"

"No!" Her voice was low but powerful. "She starts chemo again on Monday and she doesn't need this hanging over her head."

He started to object, but she placed her fingers over his mouth. "This isn't open for negotiation, Jesse. I'm not telling her. And neither are you."

His fingers wrapped around her wrist as his thumb stroked softly over her palm. "You have to promise me that you won't have anything to do with him. Ever." His voice was fierce, his eyes fiercer as they glared into hers. "I mean it, Desiree. Nothing. If that jackass so much as looks at you accidentally, I want to know about it."

"Jesse—"

"Promise me." His hands reached up, cupped her face. "Not telling your folks is against my better judgment and if you can't promise me that you'll let me protect you, Desiree, then this isn't happening. We'll go up to the house right now—"

"Okay," she said. "I promise."

He studied her, his eyes searching for something he must have found, for he nodded reluctantly. "Good enough. And I promise you he won't hurt you again, Desi. I swear, no one will ever hurt you like that again."

"Jesse—" Her voice broke and tears spilled before she could stop them.

"Shh, darlin'. Don't cry." He pulled her against him, his strong arms holding her tightly against his body. "I can't stand to see you cry."

His voice was low, strained, and his tenderness only made her weep harder. Cursing softly, he settled onto a nearby bench and pulled her onto his lap. She continued to sob, her heart aching from the bittersweet joy of being held so closely by the man she loved even as her body ached from the attack of another.

He rocked her, murmuring soothingly as he stroked her hair. "Desi, stop. Please stop. You'll make yourself sick."

But she couldn't stop as the night's events caught up with her.

He cursed again, his voice low and vicious, then his lips were skimming over her wet chin, her cheeks, up to her eyes to catch the tears before they could fall. She shuddered at the first touch of his lips, at the unbearable sweetness that came from being touched by Jesse.

Before he could move, before he could stop, she wrapped her arms around him, locking him against her. His lips moved over her cheek, again, and she turned her head slightly, just enough so that their lips met.

His lips closed over hers, gently, sweetly, and for

a moment the earth ceased to spin. Her lungs stopped breathing, her heart stopped beating—everything she was and everything she had was focused on the tentative brush of his lips against hers.

Warmth started in her belly, spread outward slowly as her body came to life for the very first time. His mouth moved against hers, once, twice and the warmth became a burning she never could have imagined. She moaned, softly, and opened her lips.

Then it was over. Jesse stood, thrusting her away from him, his breathing harsh. "Desiree—"

"It's okay."

He shoved a hand through his unrestrained hair, his movements jerky and uncoordinated for the first time since she'd met him. "I'm sorry. I don't—"

"Jesse," she interrupted, waited until his gaze found hers. She nearly smiled at the confusion in them, nearly lit up as joy coursed through her. "It's okay."

"No, it's not. I didn't mean—"

"I know."

"Desi—"

"Shh." She reached up, her fingers once again resting against his mouth. "Jesse, stop. It's okay. I understand." She paused and her thumb stroked his cheek. "Really, I do. Thank you for comforting me, for saving me. I'm okay now."

She reached down and gathered her shoes, feeling his gaze heavy upon her. She walked to the door, stopped, turned to face him. "Don't beat yourself up over this, Jesse. I was the one who kissed you."

Then she spun around and ran, full speed, toward home, knowing that her life had irrevocably changed. It might take her a few years, but Jesse Rainwater was going to be hers. He just didn't know it yet.

CHAPTER FOUR

DAMN HER TO HELL. Jesse's booted feet covered the distance from the house to the garden quickly, though he barely noticed where he was going. How could he have been so damn stupid, so goddamn gullible? He'd been softening toward her, thinking he'd made a mistake. Thinking that maybe, if he compromised a little more, things could change.

He tried not to focus on what a complete ass he'd really been. Knowing that he'd been feeling bad about the state of their marriage when all along she'd been hiring his replacement behind his back was enough to make him sick. And not only hadn't she consulted him about it, but she hadn't even had the courtesy to say a word about it. Not one damn word.

That pretty much showed what she thought of him, didn't it? Not even the courtesy of a boss/employee conference to tell him that she didn't think things were working out any longer, that she had gone and hired a new trainer to start in January. January—one month from now. One month, he assumed, so that he could show the new guy the ropes. Like hell.

He'd known—goddammit, he had known—when she'd come back from the races in Kentucky that something was up. Known that she was hiding something from him. Again. When he'd confronted her about it she'd laughed at him. Told him there was nothing wrong and that he was blowing things out of proportion.

Damn her!

It was the secrecy, more than anything else, that had made him think about divorce. He couldn't take the deceit any longer, nor could he live with the knowledge that his wife wouldn't confide in him. How had their marriage become such a sham when she was all he'd ever wanted?

He wanted to throw things, needed to hit something, was almost desperate to pick a fight just so he'd have something to throttle. Fury coursed through him, so powerful that it made him shake, nearly brought him to his knees.

It wasn't that she'd replaced him. Or, he corrected himself with habitual honesty, it wasn't just that she'd replaced him. It was that she had done so in such an incredibly devious way. That she hadn't told him. That she hadn't cared enough to worry about how and when he would find out.

Had she planned on telling him at all? Or was she

simply going to bring Tom onto the ranch and expect Jesse not to notice? Maybe she thought the fifteen years he had on her had suddenly made him senile?

He stared blindly at the perfectly decorated garden, barely seeing the hundreds of chairs arranged in rows or the flower bedecked arbor where his daughter would say her vows in a little more than three hours. With a roar of agony he lashed out, kicking the chair next to him and starting a chain reaction that knocked it into the chair next to it and so on, until half the row lay in disarray.

Cursing, he bent to pick up the chair he'd originally kicked, only to feel his legs go out from under him. Weak-kneed, shaking, he sank into the nearest upright seat, his head in his hands.

"Dad, are you all right?"

Stiffening at the sound of Dakota's voice, Jesse's heart rate accelerated as he tried to compose himself.

"I'm fine. Just a stupid accident." He stood stiffly, bent to pick up one of the fallen chairs.

"It didn't look like an accident to me," his son answered as he helped set the chairs to rights. "What's going on?"

"Nothing." Jesse reached over and ruffled Dakota's hair as he had done throughout his son's childhood. "Long day, that's all."

"The wedding hasn't even started yet. You getting

old or something?" Dakota teased as he set the last chair back onto its feet.

"Must be."

"Nah. Not you."

Dakota leaned in, gave him a strong one-armed hug and Jesse found himself swallowing the lump in his throat. Was he really considering going to Kentucky—leaving not only his wife but his children behind? He shook his head to clear the cobwebs that suddenly made thinking impossible.

"You need help with anything?"

Jesse heard the words from far away, though it took him a minute to fight through his emotions enough to comprehend them.

When he didn't answer right away, Dakota grabbed his biceps. "Are you all right? Dad?"

He shook it off, all of it—or at least buried it. The anger, the pain, the utter exhaustion. He could pull them out later and examine them when this day was over and his children were back to living their own lives.

"I'm fine. Just a little out of sorts." He forced a grin and headed toward the stables. "I can't believe I'm losing your sister. First Rio then Willow. Pretty soon it'll be you."

Dakota laughed as he fell into step next to his father, a careful arm still braced around Jesse's shoulder. "No way. Now that Willow's getting married and Rio and Brooke are talking about giving you your first grandchild, I figure I'm off the hook for a long while."

"I wouldn't count on that. You know your mother."

Dakota laughed. "I do. Well enough to know that she's so wrapped up in the ranch that she won't give me and my single status more than a passing thought for the next few years."

Jesse's smile was bitter. "Isn't that the truth?"

They walked toward the racing stables in silence for a few minutes before Dakota asked carefully, "So what was that chair thing all about?"

Jesse flushed as embarrassment hit him again—wasn't it just his luck that the one time he lost control, his son was around to see it? "Nothing. I'm working through some frustration issues, that's all."

"With Mom?"

"Excuse me?"

"Come on, Dad. You two can pretend all you want, but you didn't raise any stupid kids. We all know something's up."

"Nothing is up."

"Whatever."

"Dakota." Jesse's voice was serious.

"Yes?" Dakota stopped dead at the impatience in his father's tone.

"When your mother and I need our three children

running around in our heads, we'll let you know. Until then, stay the hell out."

"Got it," he said with a rueful grin.

"Good." Jesse smiled back. "Now I've got a couple calls to make. Why don't you do me a favor and check to make sure every horse in here's been exercised today?"

"Sure." Dakota loped off, his long-legged stride taking him effortlessly to the charts at the far end of the stable.

Walking into his office, Jesse picked up the phone and the stack of messages sitting on his desk, prepared to answer the most pressing phone calls before he headed up to the house to get dressed. But he found himself staring at Dakota as he worked, wondering just how obvious he and Desiree had been in the past couple of years.

If Dakota, who lived a couple of hundred miles away and was the least observant of their children, had noticed, what could Rio and Willow be thinking? His heart hurt at the idea that he had been nowhere near as discreet as he had thought he was, that his children had known all along that something was wrong.

But maybe that wasn't such a bad thing. He'd been worried the divorce would come as a huge shock to them, but maybe they'd been anticipating it for a while. Maybe it had seemed inevitable to everyone but him.

Desiree, despite her protestations of ignorance,

had to have known this was coming. Why else would she have hired a new trainer, if she hadn't expected things to fall apart between them?

Cursing himself and his inability to stop her from hurting him, Jesse turned to the messages and began dialing the phone. After returning the two most important phone calls—one about a horse he wanted to buy for the ranch and the other to an assistant trainer he and Desiree had discussed hiring—he crossed to Wink's stall and petted the five-year-old stallion.

Peace flowed through him as his hands sunk into the horse's long, wiry mane. His whole life might be a mess, but this, this was simple. He might not be able to communicate with his wife worth a damn, but at least he could still see what was going on with his horses.

Wink whickered softly, nudging him with his beautiful aristocratic nose. "I know, boy. I'm sorry your schedule's so off today, but Willow's getting married and everything's a bit crazy. Tomorrow will be better, I promise. Tomorrow we'll get you out for a nice long run, instead of that short little jog they gave you today."

Would he even be here tomorrow? Next week? Sadness overwhelmed him and he leaned forward, burying his face against the horse's neck and drawing strength from his old friend. He'd need every bit of strength he could find to get through the wedding and the reception without throttling Desiree.

He stroked the horse for a few minutes before turning away with a sigh. "Are you just about done, Dakota?" he asked. "It's time to head up to the house."

"I need a few more minutes, Dad. But go ahead if there's something you need to do."

There wasn't anything he needed to do, but he was unwilling to stand around looking pathetic and useless in front of his youngest son. He should run by the maternity barn and check on M.C. Though he knew everything was going as planned with the very pregnant mare, he'd feel better if he saw her with his own eyes instead of relying on what his assistant trainers told him. She was one of his favorites, after all, and the foal she carried was incredibly important to the Triple H's future.

Not that the ranch's future was really any of his business anymore. He crossed the room to stare blindly at the pictures and newspaper clippings Desiree had hung so painstakingly on the wall—here and in the study in the house. Little bits and pieces of the Triple H's history, little bits and pieces of her marriage. Too bad their feelings for each other weren't as unchanging as these small scraps of paper.

He was drawn, inexorably, to the one clipping *he'd* actually mounted on the wall. Desiree had never understood why he'd chosen this story to mount, had asked him to take it down numerous times. But he'd remained firm. Failure, his failure, was as much a part of the Triple H as the successes were. And this failure, his first really big one, still smarted after all these years.

In one of the most shocking upsets in horse-racing history, Crown Rhapsody lost the Belmont Stakes, and in doing so lost the Triple Crown many believed the horse was all but guaranteed.

After an incredible showing at both the Kentucky Derby and the Preakness, where she finished both races at least two lengths ahead of the field, the Triple H's horse's winning streak came to an end in the middle of the Belmont Stakes.

Halfway through the three-quarter-mile race, Rhapsody—who already had a commanding lead over most of the field—stumbled and fell, taking three more horses with her: Sterling's Silver, Serendipity and Pennywise. While she was not seriously injured, suffering only two sprained ankles, Serendipity suffered two broken legs, three shattered ribs and assorted other injuries while Pennywise ended up with a dislocated shoulder. Sterling's Silver, after much debate, was put down.

"While we at the Triple H, and the rest of the horse-racing community, are saddened by the loss of Sterling's Silver, we are extremely grateful that the collision did not endanger the lives of more horses," commented Jesse Rainwater, Crown Rhapsody's trainer since birth. "We look forward to a long racing career for Rhapsody and expect her to be back on the track within six weeks."

While few in the horseracing community doubt the brightness of Crown Rhapsody's future, all acknowledge that, for the Triple H, this year's Belmont Stakes will always be the one that got away.

HE LOVED THE SMELL of the track, the scent of horses and popcorn and money combining into a potent cocktail of luck. Jesse took a deep breath, absorbing the scent into his very soul before leaning forward and speaking softly into Crown Rhapsody's ear.

Always high-strung, today she was so nervous that neither Jesse, nor Herbert—the parrot that was her constant stall companion—could calm her down. Almost as if she, too, knew that this wasn't just another race. As if she knew that this was it—the race that could bring her everlasting glory and bring Jesse, if nothing else, a chance to relax from the craziness of the quest Big John had set him on nine years before. He was more than ready for a break, the chance for a little bit of peace calling to him as little else ever had.

Hailed as the greatest racehorse since Secretariat, the entire racing community had high hopes for Rhapsody—major newspapers and racing magazines across the country proclaimed that the Triple Crown would be won this year, that the outcome of the Belmont Stakes was a guaranteed certainty. Even the bookies had gotten onboard, offering some of the lowest odds on his horse that Belmont Park had ever seen.

There was no doubt in his mind that Rhapsody was capable of winning this race. She'd won the Derby by almost three lengths, leaving her competition in the dust—literally. The Preakness hadn't been any harder. She'd taken an early lead and raced to victory nearly unchallenged.

Why then was he so nervous about this race? Why was his stomach knotted and his head pounding as if the fate of the world rested on this one horse's shoulders? He'd never worried about a race before, had always done his best with breeding and training and left the rest up to the horse. Win some, lose some. That had always been his philosophy, though his horses won many more races than they lost.

But this was different. Desiree was on tenterhooks, thrilled and crazed at the idea of finally bringing the Triple Crown back to her daddy's ranch. Back to her ranch. Maybe that was where his own anxiety was stemming from—he didn't want to disappoint her, couldn't bear to see the sadness in her as the most coveted prize in horseracing slipped through their fingers again.

Taking a few deep breaths, Jesse calmed himself, centered himself, sent himself seeking within the worried and uptight mind of his very high-strung racehorse. He walked with her for a little while—in the manner his mother and grandfather had taught him so many years before. He found her fears and soothed them as best he could, comforting and reassuring her. If only his fears could be soothed as easily.

"It's time to go," Desiree's voice was higher than normal, excitement and nervousness showing on her face as she approached the stables where he and Rhapsody waited.

"She's ready." His own voice must have been tighter than he thought because Desiree smiled reassuringly as she laid a soothing hand on his shoulder.

"It'll be fine, Jesse."

He turned his head slightly, so that he could see both his wife and Rhapsody—the two most important women in his life today. "Do I look that bad?" he asked.

"Not to the rest of the world, but they don't know you like I do." She raised a second hand to his shoulders, began a gentle massage that loosened both his muscles and his stomach.

"Who'd we pull?" he asked, relaxing into the comforting pressure of her hands.

"Bill Daley." Her voice shimmered with suppressed excitement.

"Big John must be doing cartwheels."

"Pretty close."

"I bet. Daley's the best jockey riding today."

"This is it, Jesse. I can feel it—Rhapsody and the Triple H are going to make history today."

"Des—" His voice was low, cautioning.

"I know, I know." She rolled her eyes at him. "Anything can happen. Nothing's guaranteed. I get it. I do," she insisted as he raised a sardonic eyebrow in her direction. "But a girl can hope, can't she?"

"Open the gate for me, will you?" he asked, avoiding her question because he couldn't stand to say anything to raise or shatter her hopes. Things would play out how they would and the world would know the results soon enough.

The trip down to the starting gate was chaotic— filled with too many people trying to get a look at the Triple H's nearly mythical racehorse and too many reporters wanting a last-minute quote. He could feel Rhapsody tensing beside him as her nervousness and discomfort returned tenfold.

Cursing, he shouldered his way through the people as he used every ounce of his gift to keep Rhapsody calm. "She's losing it," he muttered to Desiree.

"Just a little farther," she answered, reaching out

a hand to stroke the horse's neck. "Hang on, girl. We're almost there."

Pushing their way through the throngs of excited racegoers, Jesse sighed in relief when he and Desiree finally made it to the starting gate. He'd been to a hell of a lot of races in his life, but he'd never seen this many people milling around behind the scenes. He hadn't prepared for it, hadn't prepared Rhapsody for it. He just hoped the horse didn't pay the price for his miscalculation.

The next few minutes flew by as Rhapsody's jockey, dressed in the red-and-gold silks of the Triple H, spent a little while talking to the horse before mounting up and getting the horse ready for the small, fenced starting gate that would spring open as soon as the gun went off.

Then it was time to step back, leaving Rhapsody in Bill's capable hands. Jesse's stomach churned as he walked away, his left hand clasped tightly in Desiree's right one. "Daddy's waiting for us," she murmured, pulling him toward the box seats.

"I'd rather watch from here."

"Jesse, no!" She turned to him, disappointment gleaming in her eyes. "It's hard to see from down here. Plus Daddy and his friends are expecting us. I told him we'd be up as soon as you got Rhapsody settled."

He started to argue that all he wanted was to be left alone to watch the race in peace. He had a sick feeling in the pit of his stomach, one he'd never felt before. Maybe it was just nervousness, maybe it was instinct, but he didn't think Rhapsody was going to win this race. And if she didn't, if something went wrong, he'd rather be alone to deal with the fallout. To deal with his failure, when he'd promised his wife that he wouldn't let her down again.

With a sigh, he draped an arm around her shoulders and let her lead him to the Triple H box. Filled with her father and his cronies, it was loud and crowded and exactly where Jesse didn't want to be. But Desiree was there, her sweet body pressed lovingly against his, her hand rubbing soothing circles on his tense back.

And so he tried to relax, despite the growing sickness in his stomach. Grabbing a cola—he didn't drink when one of his horses was racing—he made his way to the front of the air-conditioned box.

He listened as the announcer listed the horses in the race, his mind ticking off each of Rhapsody's competitors seconds before the names were announced. Mystic would give her the biggest threat by far—nearly as fast and just as graceful, he'd come in second in both the Derby and the Preakness.

But this was a high-stakes race, and every horse in it had the ability to win. Lucky Lily could easily steal the lead, as could Pennywise or Sterling's Silver.

The gun went off before he could second-guess the results, and adrenaline roared through him as Bill and Rhapsody took an early lead. As they rounded the first curve, Mystic was in second, though Lucky Lily was running a close and threatening third.

Heart pounding, Jesse watched in awe as Rhapsody fought off the pack to remain in first—around the first curve, the straightaway, the second curve, on and on until they'd reached the final stretch. Breath held, hand fiercely clutching Desiree's, he watched as Rhapsody flew for the finish line, a full length in front of Mystic.

Jesse turned to Desiree, smiled into her excited eyes, and in that one second everything changed. He heard a gasp from the crowd, whirled in time to see Rhapsody stumble and fall a mere five yards from the finish line. Bill jumped clear as the horse hit the ground hard and Jesse watched in horror as Rhapsody rolled, taking down three other horses before she finally came to a stop.

Then he was running, out of the box, down the two flights of stairs to ground level, hurtling over the barrier between the track and the stands. Flashing his all-access badge at the overwhelmed security guards as he flew past, he got to the sight of the collision before any of the other trainers or owners.

The four downed horses—Rhapsody, Pennywise, Serendipity and Sterling's Silver—were over-wrought, screaming in pain and fear. Pennywise had struggled to his feet, but Rhapsody, Serendipity and Sterling were still down.

He approached Rhapsody cautiously, his heart in his throat, and fear a living, breathing monster in his stomach. If she was hurt badly, if she wouldn't heal, they'd have to put her out of her misery, have to put her down though everything inside of him screamed at the injustice. She was a champion, a purebred, a noble spirit and the thought of killing her—even to save her pain—was anathema to him.

He glanced to the right, saw Bill holding his arm, a grimace of pain on his face as the first round of paramedics hit the field. But much as he liked the jockey, he was more concerned with getting the horses calmed before they hurt themselves or someone else.

Though Sterling was almost completely still, lying on his side and panting harshly, Rhapsody continued to try to struggle to her feet, whinnying in pain with every movement of her front legs.

"Shh, girl," he murmured as he approached her. "Just let me look at you. Let me check you out, baby, and we'll get you something for the pain."

The next few minutes, and hours, passed in a blur. Big John arrived, anger and disappointment evident in his every stride, but Jesse was too busy to give his father-in-law's state of mind more than a passing thought.

When he finally returned to the hotel after sitting through three sets of X rays and two veterinary exams, all Jesse wanted was a cold shower, a hot meal and some time with his wife. But when he opened the door to their suite, she and Big John were sitting on the couch, talking in low voices.

Conscious of their eyes on him and the sudden stillness of the room, Jesse closed the door behind him and walked slowly into the living room.

"Rhapsody's going to be fine," he said into the hostile silence. "Nothing's broken, but it'll take her a couple of weeks to recover from the sprains. She was still so nervous that the vet had to tranq her so that she wouldn't hurt herself. By the time I left she was pretty mellow."

Big John nodded, abruptly climbing to his feet. "Did you get the chance to look at the films? See what happened?"

"Mystic bit her, just a little nip on her left flank, but you know how sensitive Rhapsody is. It set her off."

"Shouldn't she have been trained for that? Expecting it as it happens quite a bit on the racetrack?" Though his voice held no trace of emotion, Jesse could see the accusation on his father-in-law's face, the misery on Desiree's.

"I'm not in the habit of walking up behind my horses and biting them, if that's what you're asking, John," Jesse commented.

"Your horses?" Big John answered with a deliberate cruelty. "And here I've been under the impression that they were my horses." He walked to the door. "You marry my daughter and suddenly get delusions of grandeur, Rainwater? Seeing as how it's been nine years and I still don't have a Triple Crown winner, I think that takes some nerve." He slammed out of the hotel room without another word, leaving Jesse standing with his mouth half-open and the first seeds of anger sprouting in his gut.

"What was that all about?" he demanded, turning toward Desiree as rage swept through him. "If Rhapsody hadn't fallen, he would have had his damn Triple Crown today and everyone knows it."

"But she did stumble and he doesn't have the Triple Crown." Her words were abrupt, her tone almost angry and Jesse stared at her incredulously. "Are you kidding me? You're going to blame this on me, too?"

Desiree bit her lip, stared at him through confused eyes. "I didn't say that, Jess. But what exactly do you want me to say?"

"I don't know. Why don't you tell me what you two were talking about when I got here?"

"Nothing," she spoke quickly, even as she avoided looking directly into his eyes. "We were discussing what had happened and how it could have been prevented."

Jesse's eyes narrowed. "Rhapsody's high-strung, Desi. You know that. Everyone knows that. And she was already spooked going into this thing—a nip on the rump was all it took to send her completely over the edge. It's not that hard to understand."

"But we should have been able to prevent it, to stop—"

"You mean *I* should have been able to stop it, don't you?"

"I didn't say that!"

"You didn't have to."

"Jesse, you promised my father a Triple Crown!"

"I promised your father that I would do my best to deliver one. I didn't guarantee it."

She shook her head in irritation. "Now you're splitting hairs."

"I'm splitting hairs? You're jumping all over me because a horse, who was going to win the race, stumbled and fell on the track. Don't you think that's just a little irrational?"

"Irrational?" Her voice rose with every syllable. "Look, I'm caught in the middle between you and my father and I didn't ask to be put there."

"Bullshit. Don't play the martyr, Desiree, it doesn't become you. You're in the middle because you put yourself there. I've *never* asked you to interfere between your father and me before and I'm not doing so now. You're the one who started on me the second your father left."

"He's got the right to be upset. His—"

"Are you even listening to yourself? What the hell does he have to be upset about? He should be grateful that Rhapsody is all right, that she didn't break both her front legs like Sterling's Silver. That he didn't have to put down a million-dollar racehorse and that she'll be able to run again." Fury ate at him, raising his voice and his blood pressure.

"Of course he's happy that Rhapsody is okay."

"Yeah. He looked really relieved when I told him."

"You're not being fair."

"I'm getting blamed because a horse fell in the race and you think I'm not being fair?"

"She didn't *win*, Jess."

"So what, Desiree? It's just a race. One that your father—and apparently, you—are completely obsessed with, but it's still just a race."

"It's more than that. Daddy wants this more that anything, has worked for it his entire life. Why can't you see that?"

"Why can't you see that he's obsessed? That his desire to win this stupid thing is almost sick?"

"Don't say that about him! Don't you ever say that! Since Mama died, this ranch is all he has. He wants to leave a legacy, Jesse. Why is that so hard for you to understand?"

Jesse laughed, but it was an angry sound. "He's already got a legacy, darlin'. Hell, he's got a dynasty. But it's not enough." He grabbed her by the arms, made her look at him. "Nothing will ever be enough. Even if he had won the Triple Crown today, he'd want another one next year. If one's good, two would be better. Or three or four… The Triple H could be the first horse ranch to ever win the Triple Crown two years in a row. Wouldn't he love that?"

She wrenched away from him. "You're being ridiculous."

"At least I'm in good company."

She stiffened, then turned and walked into the bathroom. As he listened to the click of the lock, Jesse gritted his teeth and tried desperately to keep from punching something. He hadn't meant to argue with Desiree, hadn't planned to say anything about her father at all.

But what was he supposed to do? He'd given this ranch everything he had for the past nine years. What else could she expect from him?

How could he have anticipated Rhapsody falling? What could he have done about it, even if he had seen it coming? Thrusting his hands into his hair, Jesse paced back and forth, agony and anger battling within him as he waited for Desiree to re-emerge from her self-imposed exile.

But when she finally came out of the bathroom, her face scrubbed clean and her pajamas on, he was no closer to finding a solution to their dilemma. When she came up behind him and slipped her arms around his waist, he tried to relax into her embrace but their fight was still too raw in his mind.

"I love you." She pressed her lips against the back of his neck as she slid her hands up his back and began to massage his shoulders.

He reached up, grabbed one of her hands in his own. "I love you, too, Desiree. But this isn't working. I can't live like this."

She stiffened against him. "What does that mean?"

He turned, pulling her suddenly unyielding body into his arms. "It means that I feel as torn as you do. I'm stuck in this catch-22 between the ranch and you and your father and I don't think it's healthy for any of us."

He took a deep breath, his hands running in soothing circles on her back. "I think I need to look for another job, find another ranch to train horses for."

"Jesse, no!' Her hands flew to her mouth. "You can't do that."

His eyes were grim as he studied her. "Then tell me what to do, Desiree. How do we solve this? Because I can't spend the rest of my life caught between my boss and my wife."

CHAPTER FIVE

STRIDING ACROSS THE manicured lawns of the Triple H, Desiree struggled to shake off the memories that had her in their untenable grip. The journal was in the front pocket of her coat. She'd been unable to put it away, though she knew it was both stupid and masochistic to carry it with her.

As she walked, she surveyed the lands that she had run—almost single-handedly—for the past nineteen years. She hadn't needed to do it that way; the ranch was full of qualified people who would have been more than happy to share the burden. Jesse, Don, Roman were just a few of the brilliant horsemen the Triple H employed. They'd all offered their help on too many occasions to count, yet she'd rarely taken them up on it. The ranch was hers—her inheritance, her responsibility, her pride and joy.

Even Big John hadn't tried to manage all of the day-to-day runnings of the ranch—preferring to hire the best possible people and leave it in their competent hands. She knew, had always known, that his way—at least on this—was the right way. But then, her father hadn't had anything to prove. He hadn't been the first woman to ever inherit the ranch, hadn't had half the American horseracing community watching, waiting for him to fail. He had never known what it was to be doubted, not because of decisions he made or failures he'd caused, but because of something as fundamentally unchangeable as gender.

She did know and she lived with the fear of failing every day of her life. The fear of not being good enough, of not living up to the legacy her father and grandfather and great-grandfather had left for her.

But things were changing. *She* was changing. She thought, again, of the plans she'd made for the future, of the papers she'd had drawn up and the talk she'd wanted to have with Jesse. It had been too long in coming—she knew that—but she had figured better late than never. She'd had something to prove when she'd taken over the ranch, and she liked to believe she'd proven it. Now was the time for a new era, the time for her to follow her conscience and do what was right. To do what she should have done long, long ago.

Or at least that's what she'd had planned, before Jesse had turned everything upside down.

Her shoulders drooped as she headed toward the maternity barn—Majesty's Child was set to foal anyday now, and she wanted to check on her, make sure she was being taken care of. She—and Jesse, of course—had great hopes for this foal. Both its parents were descendents of the greatest racing lines in history, and she had a feeling—a tingling in her blood, in her soul—that told her this horse was the one. This was the one that would finally realize her father's dream, her own dream, of bringing a Triple Crown to the ranch.

The caterer's van pulled up, and she knew that she didn't need to meet them, that Maria would set things in motion. But she wanted to check with them to make sure everything was as Willow wanted it. Desiree also needed to talk to the florist who was, even now, building the arbor of poinsettias and mistletoe that Willow and James would be married under. There was also the hairdresser. Felipe was nothing if not arrogant and insecure enough to demand her fawning attention.

But all that could wait. First M.C. She entered the barn slowly, savoring the joy that came every time she entered this particular stable. She loved all of her horses, loved all aspects of running the Triple H. But there was something special about this stable, about the anticipation, the becoming that touched her deeply. Like the training circles, this part of the ranch was all about possibilities, about what might be, what could be, if hard work, talent and a little luck struck the right combination.

Her eyes narrowed as she looked around—the stable was empty of ranch workers, though she'd given specific orders that M.C. not be left alone. No one deserved to go through labor alone—horse or human—and that went double for the Triple H's best hope for the future.

Striding purposefully over to M.C.'s stall, she reached for the walkie-talkie she kept clipped to her belt at all times and prepared to blast Don, her stable manager, out of the water.

But as her finger went to depress the button, she stopped abruptly. A deep and gentle crooning came from the stall, a sound she knew well, as it was one she'd heard her husband make innumerable times.

M.C. wasn't alone. Jesse was with her.

Jesse was here.

She swallowed, concentrated on breathing through the chaos of too many emotions. She wasn't ready yet, didn't know what to say, what to do. She'd known she'd have to face him, but she'd figured it would be later—when her makeup and hair were flawless, when she was dressed for the wedding and her armor was firmly in place.

She'd never imagined that it would be here, that it would be now. Should she walk away or stay and ride things out?

Her shoulders squared suddenly and anger burned in the pit of her stomach. She was a lot of things, but she wasn't a coward. And she had no reason to fear this confrontation. He was the one who'd been low enough to ask for a divorce on their daughter's wedding day. He was the one who'd lived with her for days and weeks, maybe even months, while he plotted to divorce her without bringing the subject up even once.

No, she wouldn't run and she wouldn't cry. She'd shed enough tears today, more than she'd thought she was capable of crying. She refused to give him the satisfaction of knowing how completely he'd leveled her.

"How is she?" Her voice wasn't as strong as she might have liked, but it was steady.

He didn't look up. "Ready to go into labor. I'm pretty sure it'll be tomorrow if it isn't later today."

"You've arranged for someone to be with her, right? When you and I are at the wedding?"

His head jerked up. For a moment she saw pain and hostility move in the depths of his eyes before the increasingly familiar shutters came down, hiding everything inside him.

"Yes, Desiree." His voice was ice-cold. "I know what you have riding on this colt. And even if you hadn't pinned your hopes on it, I'm still trainer enough to know not to leave a laboring mare alone."

She flushed, embarrassed despite herself. "I didn't mean—"

He snorted as he rose to his feet, stepping lithely

around the bulky mare. "I know exactly what you meant, darlin'."

Her spine stiffened at the sarcastic endearment. "Look, I don't know what your problem is—"

"As of two hours ago, I don't have any problems." He shrugged. "Things are definitely looking up."

For a moment shock held her mind and body immobile. Desiree stared at him, slack-jawed, as his words echoed through her. She tried to speak, but his contempt froze every part of her, including her tongue.

"Excuse me. I've got work to do." Jesse headed for the door.

It was his movement that unfroze her, his ability to ignore her that had her going after him before she could think better of it. "You bastard! You no-good, unbelievable bastard!"

"Don't start, Desiree," he said as he continued walking.

"What do you expect me to do, Jesse? Just stand here with my mouth shut like a good little girl? Just sign the papers without any discussion, any explanation?"

He stopped, pinned her with those obsidian eyes. "I thought things were pretty clear."

"Clear? You throw an envelope at me, tell me to sign what's inside and head for the door? What's clear about that, Jesse? What's honest or decent or right about it?"

"You're going to talk to me about decency? I've

spent thirty-three years of my life on this ranch, taking your shit, cleaning up your messes. I'm done with it, Desiree. Finished."

"Thirty-three years? The first five I was too young to do anything but follow you around like a puppy dog! And for the last twenty-seven I've been your *wife*."

"You've been my *boss*. From the moment your father died, something changed in you. Something fundamental. And it's continued to change, continued to warp until I hardly recognize you. Until I hardly recognize us!"

She actually saw red, his words causing a fine red mist to float in front of her eyes. "Your boss? Are we back to that again? My God, Jesse. We're partners. We've always been partners."

His laugh was harsh and painful to hear. "You don't know what partnership is, darlin'. You never have. It's all or nothing with you and it always has been. And I'm tired of being nothing in your eyes."

Her hand flew to her mouth as shock rocked through her. "Is that what you think?"

"It's what I know." His hands clenched into fists. "You want to do everything, you want everything your own way. You don't listen to anyone with a different opinion, including me. That's not a partnership, Desiree. That's a dictatorship."

He ran his hands through his hair. "You're good at game-playing, good at acting like you care what I think, what Don and Roman and Jo think. But the truth is, you do what you want and to hell with anyone else."

"That's not true!" Fear and horror battered her from the inside, but her eyes were dry as she faced him down. "I make decisions because I have to. It's my ranch, Jesse. My responsibility."

"Exactly. *Your* ranch." He nodded, even as a look of loathing crossed his face. "And if you read the papers I gave you, you know I don't want a damn thing from you or this ranch except my freedom. Then you won't even have to pretend to share."

"Why are you doing this? Saying those things to me when—" Her voice broke as she sucked air into her suddenly starved lungs.

"Are you even listening to yourself? I'm not doing this to you, Desiree. I'm doing it for us. We've lived in our sham of a marriage long enough. It's time to move on."

"Now our marriage is a sham? Twenty-seven years and three kids later you're telling me this?" she snapped before she could stop herself. "You've got nerve."

"And you've got a chip on your shoulder a mile wide. It's gotten so big that I can't even find you under it anymore, let alone find a way to walk around it." He grabbed her by the arms, pulled her up on tiptoe until her eyes were nearly level with his.

He was so close she could see the ring of black

surrounding the dark coffee of his eyes, could feel his breath mingling with hers. Her heart beat erratically, but before she could do anything but blink, he said, "I can't do this anymore. I want out."

He set her back on her feet and turned away without another word.

She called after him, but he didn't respond, didn't turn around, didn't acknowledge that he heard her even as she screamed his name.

Her sorrow—and the journal in her pocket— weighed her down more than she'd ever thought possible.

I spent the next two years following Jesse around, waiting for him to notice me, to remember that one brief kiss that had changed my life. In my single-mindedness, I was blind to so much around me—the young men who wanted more than friendship, the excitement of the world outside of the Triple H, the sickness my mother tried desperately to keep hidden. I was so self-absorbed that I missed it all—until the October of my nineteenth year.

Two months before I turned twenty, my eyes were finally opened. Too soon to escape un- scathed. Too late to do any good. I woke from my self-indulgent trance in time to watch my mother die.

She died on October twenty-seventh. Two days before, I stood over her bed and searched for some remnant of the woman I had known. Some small spark that told me this was my mama, the woman who loved me more than anyone on earth.

I couldn't find her. Not in the pain-filled eyes or the dull and lifeless hair. Not in the cloying smell of the sick room that had long since overpowered the scent of Mama's favorite perfume. And no matter how hard I searched, I couldn't find my mother in the skeleton on the bed. She had shrunk and shrunk until there was nothing left of her, nothing but a shell that was totally unrecognizable.

I often wondered if she'd made such a big deal of my prom because she'd known she wouldn't be around for my wedding. Had she known, even then, that she would lose the battle with cancer? Had she suffered through round after round of the chemotherapy my father insisted upon, knowing the entire time that the treatment wasn't working? Had she listened to my father's words of encouragement, to my own words, and kept her pain to herself so as not to disappoint us?

I held her hand, gently, until she fell asleep then I ran out into the inky darkness of the midnight ranch. I ran from the rage, from the wild grief that seared me. I ran from my impotence, from my inability to change anything that mattered. I ran from the past. I ran from the future. I ran and ran and ran.

LEFT, RIGHT. LEFT, RIGHT. Desiree focused on the rhythmic pounding of her feet as she ran, focused on the task of putting one foot in front of the other. Focused on the cement, gravel and grass that she passed over. Focused on the wildflowers and trees that she ran through as she struggled to leave the house and everything inside it far behind.

Left, right. Left, right. The Rolling Stones blasted from her Walkman, beat in her head as she continued to put one foot in front of the other. She covered miles in the darkness—ignoring the stitch in her side and the hitch in her breath—heading blindly toward the only sanctuary she had left. Panic and pain crawled though her, leaving her so weak that when she finally reached the watering hole she could barely stand. Falling to her knees, she pressed her forehead into the ground as her fingers clawed at the rich, brown earth. Her heart beat fiercely, throbbing in her chest and her ears and her veins, drowning out everything but the knowledge that this really was the end.

Curling into a ball, she wrapped her arms around

herself and held on tight. If she let go, even for one second, she knew that she would shatter into so many pieces that she might never be whole again.

Burrowing her face into the crook of her elbow, Desiree stifled the screams, refusing to give in to the hot tears beating against her closed eyes. Hoarse sounds wrenched from her throat as she rocked back and forth, praying for the control her parents had always expected. As she prayed for acceptance and a miracle that she knew wouldn't come.

Mama's dead. Mama's dead. Mama's dead. The mantra beat in her head. Though Mama had yet to take her last breath, Desiree knew the time she had left could be measured in hours instead of days. Desiree choked on the sobs she refused to release. She ripped off her headphones, for the first time in her life choosing silence over the music that consumed her waking minutes.

Suddenly he was there. Jesse dropped to his knees next to her, folding her into his arms, holding her against his hard chest. His beloved scent—a combination of horses, heat and rain—enveloped her, stealing past the last of her defenses. After the days and years of waiting, his embrace was so unexpected that it shattered her control.

"Mama's gone," she sobbed, wrapping her arms around his neck and holding on as tightly as she could. "She's gone, Jesse. And I can't get her back."

His arms cradled her and his hands stroked her back as he rocked her.

"Shh, darlin'," he murmured softly into her hair. "Shh, I know."

"Why didn't I see it? Why didn't *I* know?" She tried to pull away, but his grip tightened, keeping her tear-soaked face pressed against him.

"It's not your fault, Desiree."

"I should have spent more time with her. I should have seen how bad she was." Her grief made her voice and the words she said nearly unrecognizable.

"She didn't want you to see, darlin'. I don't think she wanted you to know until after she was gone."

"She is gone, Jesse! She is. That poor shell isn't Mama." Completely hysterical now, she never questioned how Jesse had found her, how he'd known that she needed him. She just held tight and poured all of her anger and grief and impotence into him.

And he took it. He held her through the onslaught, stroking her hair and rubbing her back in soothing circles. Murmuring gentle words of comfort in her ear. Sheltering her close to his chest, protecting her from herself and her out-of-control emotions.

When the storm passed, she lay against him, his heartbeat steady and comforting beneath her cheek. It was a long time before Desiree blocked the sorrow enough to become aware of where she was and who she was with.

As reality slowly intruded, she stiffened against Jesse, embarrassed and confused. She tried to pull away, but his arms held her in place. "Don't," he murmured.

"Don't what?" she asked, looking up at him through her lashes.

"Don't leave. Let me hold you a little longer."

His words startled her, mixed with the rage and love that warred within. She escaped while she still had the strength. "Why didn't you tell me?"

He didn't pretend to misunderstand. "They didn't want you to know."

"Why?" she demanded, her hands fisting. "Why could everyone else know and not me? There I am at school, going to classes and parties, hanging out with my friends, thinking everything is fine. I called home almost every day, damn you! I talked to you, to Daddy, to *her*. None of you said a damn word to me about her getting sicker. None of you told me *anything!*" Her voice was too loud, but she couldn't lower it, just as she couldn't stop the pain-filled words spewing forth.

"It wasn't up to me to tell you." His voice was low and firm, but he reached a hand out to her.

She felt him grab her hand as if from far away, felt his long, hard fingers smooth gently over her wrist, over her palm. "That's a cop-out, Jesse, and you know it. A pathetic excuse that doesn't mean anything. You don't care about me at all. You couldn't care and lie to me the way you did."

He stiffened, withdrew his hand. She couldn't see his expression in the dark, but she heard his indrawn breath, saw his shoulders tense and straighten against her assault. "You would have come home and sat with her and cared for her. And you would have died a little bit each day as you watched her fade. Your father didn't want that for you."

"It wasn't his choice."

He inclined his head. "Maybe not. But it was *her* choice. She made it very clear to your father, and Big John made it very clear to me. She didn't want you to know."

"She's my mother, Jesse. She's my mother!"

He sighed, reached for her again. She struggled, tried to evade him, but his hands remained on her arms. "Have you ever thought of it from her point of view? Ever considered that maybe she couldn't stand for you to see her like that? Couldn't stand to know that your last memory of her would be a painwracked shell of her former self?

"She loved you, Desiree, loved you enough to live without you these last few months, though you would have brought her comfort. Can't you love her enough to understand? To forgive her?"

The words hit with the force of a sledgehammer.

Shame nearly leveled her, making her flush and turn away from Jesse.

"I didn't—" Her voice broke and she steadied it. "I didn't think of it like that."

"Of course you didn't." He wrapped her slight, cold body inside the shelter of his large, warm one. "Just as she didn't think of it from your point of view. Whether she was right or wrong, it's done, Desiree. We can't go back from here."

"I'm not ready to lose her, Jesse."

"I know, darlin'."

She tried to hold herself away from him, to stay tense and removed. But his warmth was insidious, winding itself around and inside of her until she melted against him.

They stayed that way for a long time—Jesse sheltering her against the fierce emotions ripping through her. Beneath his touch, her riotous emotions finally quieted, giving her a chance to think, to reason.

"I'm sorry—"

"Don't."

She sighed. "Jesse."

"No." He shook his head, his voice firm. "Don't apologize and don't be embarrassed. There's nothing for you to be ashamed of here."

"I am sorry. I didn't mean to say those things—"

"I said, don't." He shifted enough to look her in

the eyes. "Desiree, you have a right to grieve for your mother. You don't ever need to apologize for that."

"I wasn't." The words came out stiff and formal. "I was apologizing for—" She searched desperately for the right word. "For saying those things. For treating you badly. For…inconveniencing you." Her voice trailed away as she saw felt him tense against her.

"Inconveniencing? That's what you call this?"

She shrank from his anger, suddenly defenseless. "I just thought—"

"What?" He grasped her chin in his hand, forced her to look at him. "Desiree, don't you know what you mean to me?"

For one blinding moment, everything else disappeared. "No." Her voice was little more than a whisper.

His eyes narrowed. "No what? You don't know? Or you don't want to know?"

Her heart stuttered in her chest. She wanted to speak but didn't know what to say. As she stared into them, she saw something she'd never seen before. It sent shivers down her spine and created a strange heat between her thighs. She lifted one trembling hand to his face and ran her thumb over his mouth before she could stop herself. "Jesse."

It was a plea and he knew it, though she barely understood what she was asking for. He cupped her face, his touch soothing and arousing at the same time. She closed her eyes, nervous, excited, determined to savor every second of contact.

"Look at me, Desiree." Though his voice was low, it was no less an order. "I want to see your eyes when I do this."

Slowly, so slowly that time seemed to stop, he lowered his lips to hers. Desiree's heart thudded painfully in her chest and, for a moment, she forgot to breathe. He was going to kiss her. Jesse Rainwater was finally, finally going to kiss her. Not a simple brush of lips, like that long-ago moment in the barn, but a real kiss. Her lips parted of their own volition and though her eyes wanted desperately to close, she kept them opened, terrified that he would stop if she broke the spell.

Jesse stopped when his lips were barely an inch from hers. She willed him to come closer, to move that one last inch. But he didn't. Instead he waited. Waited while his thumb stroked over her cheek. Waited while his eyes stared into hers. Waited until her nerves were frazzled, her body was taut and desire thrummed through her with every beat of her heart.

"Jesse," she pleaded, breathless and achy.

"Desiree," he answered, his voice tight and aroused.

"Now. Please, now," she said, uncaring that she was almost begging.

He grinned darkly as he bridged the distance

between them. "Now," he agreed, just before his mouth covered hers.

Light exploded in front of her dazzled eyes, and need, sharp and painful, swept through her, buckling her knees before she could brace herself. She stumbled against him and Jesse held her more tightly, his arms strong and firm around her.

His lips moved against hers, coaxing her to open her mouth. She did and was instantly rewarded with more sensations than she'd thought it possible to feel. Soft. Warm. Deep. She sighed, cuddled closer and hung on for dear life.

He sipped from her. Devoured her. Absorbed her, until heat slammed through her and dizziness circled. His tongue brushed her top lip, traced her bottom lip, plunged inside and tasted her.

Desiree moaned and shut her eyes as the world spun. This, she thought as his tongue swept softly over hers. This is what she'd been waiting for. This is what she'd always known she would feel.

He pulled away, cupped her face in his hands. "Jesse." Her voice was soft, dreamy, as she moved to recapture his lips.

"Desiree." His was harsh, tight. "Let me take you home."

"Jesse, no!" It was almost a wail. "Please."

"Not here, darlin'." His lips brushed against hers, comforting and arousing at the same time. "Not now."

"Why not now?" she demanded, cupping his face in her hands and leaning into another kiss. Desiree could feel his resistance—and his desire—in the heat pumping from his body, could feel his inner struggle in the hands that refused to move from her shoulders.

He was shaking his head as he pulled his lips reluctantly from hers. "This can't be because of what's happening, Desiree." He paused for a moment, as if he didn't want to continue. "It can't be because of your mother."

"It's not!"

"How do you know?" His gaze held hers captive, demanded the truth.

She wanted to yell, to pout, to beg. But he was right and she knew it. She would never forgive herself if their first time was on her mother's deathbed, no matter how much she wanted the cessation of pain his touch promised her.

But what happened next? she wondered. How could she learn to let her mother go? What would become of Jesse and her? She closed her eyes, blocking out the insidious darkness of the night as question after question bombarded her.

CHAPTER SIX

JESSE STORMED INTO HIS office, closing the door with enough force to rattle the frames on the wall. One fell to the ground, the glass shattering into hundreds of tiny pieces.

Like his marriage. Like him, without Desiree.

Fury grabbed him by the throat. He reached for the bottle of Crown Royal—ha, ha—that Dakota had given him for his birthday this year. His sixty-fourth birthday. Christ, when had he gotten so damn old?

He poured himself a finger, tossed it back like water. Poured two fingers this time and settled into his desk chair to brood. Despite the silver liberally sprinkling his hair and the deep grooves near his eyes, he didn't feel sixty-four. His body still worked the way it was supposed to—his back was strong, his mind agile. But recently time seemed to be creeping up on him and he had begun to wonder how much of it he had left.

There were so many things he hadn't done yet,

things he'd put off as he chased after Big John's dream, after Desiree's dream. A dream that seemed more impossible and less important with every season that passed.

Desiree didn't understand. Maybe she couldn't—at forty-nine, time hadn't started ticking away from her in the same way it suddenly had for him. Maybe it never would. As young and as vibrant as she'd ever been, Desiree rolled over every obstacle in her path. Getting older wasn't important, didn't have anything to do with her goals for the ranch, so she didn't pay attention to it or even acknowledge it.

He took another sip of his drink, savoring the warmth spreading through him. He'd been cold for so long that the sudden fire felt like heaven. Fire from the liquor. Fire from Desiree.

She was a mess—more shell-shocked and upset than he'd seen her in years. Of course, that wouldn't last long. And when the shock wore off she'd come gunning for him in a way that made their earlier encounter look like a little girl's tea party. Some small part of him almost looked forward to it.

Desiree. His *loving* wife, the mother of his children. Why the hell hadn't she said something when he'd moved out of their room eight months before? Or if not then, then anytime during the ensuing months? A little open communication, a small expression of concern, anything, really, and he would have run back to her and tried to make things better. Tried to be a better trainer, a better husband. That was the power she had over him, the power she'd always had.

Despair swept through him, though he cursed himself for being an idiot, a moron, a stupid fool. After thirty-three years, the independent horse trainer who'd shown up here knowing he was the best was long gone. In his place was a much more humble man, one who'd tasted failure too many times to think he had all the answers. These days, much of his self-worth was tied to his feelings for Desiree, while much of hers was tied to her feelings for the ranch.

The glass flew across the room before he was conscious of throwing it. He watched impassively as the heavy crystal tumbler shattered against the big stone fireplace in the corner.

He'd failed her, damn it. He'd failed his children, failed the ranch and even failed her father, though the son-of-a-bitch was the only one who actually deserved it. But Desiree didn't deserve it, had never deserved it, and neither had his kids. Though the Triple Crown had never meant much to his children, he'd wanted one of his horses to win it for them. So they could have their father back. So he wouldn't have to work so hard to win something that was nearly impossible.

So they could have their mother back.

Every season that passed without the crown saw Desiree working harder, longer, more determined than ever to prove that she deserved this ranch. As if anyone had ever doubted her capability. But Desiree didn't see the admiration in the faces of her employees, or the awe directed at her from so many in the racing community as her horses won race after important race.

Unable to bear the stillness of inactivity a second longer, Jesse stood to pace. He was still too wound up to face the others, still too raw to face his wife.

He grimaced. His soon-to-be ex-wife. Had he been stupid to think divorce was the only answer? God knew he still loved Desiree, still wanted her, still needed her as much as, if not more than, he had all those years ago when she'd been too young and too beautiful for him.

HE'D WALKED OUT ON her again.

In the thirty-three years she'd known Jesse, he'd never treated her with even a hint of disrespect. Now, today, he'd managed to heap a mountain of it on her—not once but twice.

She stared around the maternity barn in disbelief. Was she really that bad? Had she really done everything he'd accused her of? She'd shared the ranch—of course she had. She was in the position to know, better than anyone, just how much the Triple H needed Jesse. Without him these last few decades, they'd be so much less than what they were.

She knew how to be a partner—

She cut off the train of thought abruptly, refusing to give Jesse the power to make her second-guess herself any more than she already had. Even so, she was left with the same question that had been running through her head for the past few hours. What happened now?

"Are you okay, Mom?"

She jumped at the unexpected voice, whirled around to find herself face-to-face with her oldest son. Rio. Love swept through her, even as she sought to hide her anguish. Rio was, and always had been, their most perceptive and compassionate child. Not to mention the best veterinarian the Triple H had ever employed.

"I'm fine, sweetheart. Just thinking."

"About Willow?" he asked, as he slipped an arm around her shoulders in a quick hug. Despite his embrace, she sensed a distance between them. It was a distance she herself had put there, one she'd had cause to regret almost every day for the past nine years. She'd made one mistake too many with her oldest child and now she was paying the consequences. They all were.

"About change." She smiled, laid a hand on his cheek. "I love you."

His eyes grew shadowed, his voice cooler. "I love

you, too, Mom. But that doesn't explain why you look so sad."

She shrugged, turning her head away before he could study her anymore. What could she say to him? *I'm sad because your father hates me? Because he handed me divorce papers today and wasted no time telling me how much contempt he has for me? Because you don't love me the way you used to and I don't know how to fix all the mistakes that I've made?* Somehow, she didn't think that was the best way to approach Rio, let alone explain the divorce to their three children.

The divorce. Had she just thought about it as if it was a foregone conclusion? As if there were no other options, nothing left to fight for? And why should she have to explain the divorce at all—Jesse was the one who wanted it. Let him explain to their children that he no longer loved her. Let him come up with a good reason to explain bailing out of a twenty-seven year marriage. Let him…

She stopped abruptly. Unless he already had a good reason. Unless he already had her replacement lined up. Could that be it? Did Jesse have another woman?

Nausea rose, nearly choking her, but logic couldn't be denied. It made sense, would explain his absence in her bed and the sudden urgency of his demands. How could she have missed it?

"Mom?" Rio interrupted her musings.

With a conscious effort she pushed the thoughts

away, forcing herself to focus on her son instead of the horror cutting through her. "Did you come to check out M.C.?" she asked.

"Yeah. Before I have to change into the monkey suit James picked out for us." He opened the medical bag at his feet, pulled out his stethoscope. "How's she doing?"

"Your dad thinks she'll foal today, tomorrow at the latest."

Rio crouched down and ran his big, gentle hands along the mare's belly before listening with his stethoscope. His concentration was intense, his dark brown eyes far away as he examined one of his favorite patients.

Desiree watched as he rolled up his sleeves, treating the mare tenderly. Desiree had done something right in the past twenty-seven years, something to be proud of. And he was standing right in front of her. He had inherited his father's gift and used it in the best possible way. It was hard to believe she'd ever objected to his chosen profession.

"Looks like Dad's right," he commented as he finished his examination. "As usual."

He crossed to the sink, washed up. "So has Willow completely lost her mind yet?"

"Not yet. But it's close."

"I can imagine." He grinned. "It's hard to believe the little brat's actually getting married."

Desiree smiled, nodded. "It's hard to believe you three are all grown up, with lives of your own."

"Change is good, Mom. Now maybe you and Dad can concentrate on something besides the ranch and us."

She turned to stare into the wise eyes of her oldest child. "What's that supposed to mean?' She tried to sound carefree but knew she'd failed.

"I don't have to live here to know something's not right with you and Dad, you know. It's written all over your face."

Oh God. Did everyone see it? Had everyone known but her? Her mind raced to come up with an answer as she picked her way through her own confusion and hurt to explain things to her oldest son.

"Don't worry about it, Mom. I'm not asking for a play-by-play of your problems. I just thought that, with the wedding over, you might be able to spend some time on them. You and Dad. A New Year's resolution or something."

"Is it so obvious, then?"

He fed M.C. a carrot from his pocket. He was quiet so long, she didn't think he was going to answer. Then he said, "I don't know. I just remember how things used to be. You know, when you and Dad were a team, instead of two people with separate agendas and separate lives."

Those days haunted her. Days when Jesse couldn't

get enough of her—when he showed up wherever she was just to say hi, just to steal a kiss and a few minutes alone with her.

She sighed heavily as she reached a hand out to stroke her son's hair. Those days were long gone, replaced by hours of anger, weeks of silence, months without making love.

Rio was right. Jesse was right. Somewhere, somehow, things had gone so terribly wrong. But she could still remember the day everything had first been set right.

Things have always come easy to me—some say I've been blessed while others claim I've lived a charmed life. In some ways, I guess they're right. Everything I've ever wanted, I've gotten—either from my parents or through my own sheer, stubborn determination. There's never been an obstacle I couldn't go over or around, never been one that I couldn't knock down.

Until Jesse. After Mama's death, I expected things to change for us, expected our relationship to be different. It was different, all right. While my role remained the same—I still sought out Jesse at every opportunity—his role had changed. Suddenly he wanted nothing to do with me—the casual hugs disappeared, as did the late-night chats in the stables and the smiles that lit me up from the inside.

Oh, he stuck by me through Mama's funeral, let me lean on him, let me take comfort and strength from him. But by the time I left for school—a few days after Mama's funeral—he was nowhere to be seen. I couldn't even find him to say goodbye.

This pattern continued for the next two and a half years—as I finished my sophomore, junior and senior years in college. When I went home on school vacations, I rarely saw him— he always managed to be somewhere other than where I expected him to be. Somewhere away from me. That first year after Mama died was probably the worst of my life—not only had I lost my mother, but I'd lost my best friend as well. And I didn't even know why.

As the months passed, I spent hours analyzing my last moments alone with Jesse. Spent hours wondering what I'd done wrong. Had I been too needy? Too inexperienced? Too forward? Too desperate? Too what? The questions haunted me, coloring my experiences with other men.

Not that I wanted another man. Jesse had been the only man I'd ever noticed from the time I was sixteen, and nothing had changed, despite his obvious discouragement. But I was determined. His rejection was merely one more challenge, one more obstacle on the road my life was supposed to follow. And as soon as I figured out what I had done to turn him away, I could fix it. Fix me. Until he couldn't help but see me, want me, need me as much as I wanted and needed him.

Big John brought me home the day after my college graduation—he was the only one who came to the ceremony, as Jesse sent a very polite note declining my invitation to attend. A note that I ripped to pieces as I stormed around my one-bedroom apartment.

Daddy wanted to send me to Europe for a month as a graduation present—a present I declined. I'd already been away from the Triple H for far too long and I was desperate to be back. Desperate to work with the horses again and desperate to see Jesse, though I was deathly afraid he didn't feel the same way about me.

But I was twenty-two, optimistic and reasonably attractive—I was what you might call a late-bloomer. I'd finally grown into my long limbs and big feet, had finally developed the confidence to wear my bright-red hair with pride rather than apology. More than that, I was determined. I'd never given up on anything

I'd wanted in my whole life and I wasn't about to start now—not with Jesse, who was more important to me than anyone on earth.

So I plotted and planned, using the time that Jesse was at races as a chance to get myself ready for the battle to come. It was my last stand, my final attack, and I refused to even imagine what life would be like if it didn't work.

DESIREE STEPPED BACK and surveyed the apartment, excitement and nervousness warring within her as she put her plan into action. The changes she'd made to Jesse's place were subtle but important. The lights were dimmed—she'd had to change the bulbs to get the desired effect—and her homemade Alfredo sauce simmered in the kitchen, filling the apartment with the tantalizing smells of garlic and cream. The salad was tossed, the pasta boiling and dessert was in the fridge, where a couple of bottles of truly excellent Chianti waited.

Music played in the background—Van Morrison crooning about his brown-eyed girl. Desiree had set the table for two, using dishes and a tablecloth she'd bought in college. Though the urge had been strong to decorate with flowers and candles, she'd fought against it. They were obvious, too obvious when she was hoping to sneak up on his blind side.

She smiled with satisfaction as she caught sight of

herself in the mirror on the far wall. While she'd kept everything in the apartment understated, relaxed, she'd dressed with anything but subtlety in mind.

Her dress was red—bright, fire-engine red—as were the bra and panties beneath it. And while it had long sleeves and a modest neckline, it clung lovingly to her every curve. Her shoes were stilettos—impractical and sexy, they showed off her rider's legs to great advantage.

She checked to make sure her hair and makeup were as close to perfection as she could get them. It was after eight o'clock and Jesse should be here any minute. He usually stopped working about this time every night, or at least took a break before heading back out. But if things went according to plan tonight, Jesse wouldn't leave the apartment before morning. And neither would she.

Footsteps sounded on the stairs outside and panic crawled sickly through her stomach. This was it, her last chance. If he rejected her now…

Forcing any negative thoughts to the back of her mind, Desiree flew to the kitchen and stirred the sauce, trying desperately to look as normal as possible under the circumstances. As if it was normal for her to be cooking in Jesse's house, dressed to the nines.

She heard the door open and his footsteps come to an abrupt halt. Taking a deep breath, she turned, smiling, to greet the man she was determined to spend the rest of her life with.

He was frowning, his eyes narrow and suspicious as he examined the small table set for two. His gaze met hers from across the room, anything but welcoming.

For a second her courage deserted her and she had to fight the urge to run as fast and as far as her skinny heels would carry her. Then she noticed the quick flicker in his eyes, the spark of desire that came and went so quickly she might have imagined it.

"Hey, Jesse." She approached him.

"Desiree. What are you doing here?"

"We haven't said more than ten words to each other since I got back from school a few months ago. I thought it was past time that we caught up."

He raised an eyebrow sardonically. "Caught up, huh?"

She flushed. "Absolutely." She gestured to the kitchen. "I made dinner. I thought we could talk while we ate."

He stalked toward her. "What is it, exactly, that you want to talk about, Desiree?" His voice was low, unnerving.

She shrugged, forced a laugh, tried desperately to look and sound unconcerned. "You. The horses. The ranch. Whatever."

This time both eyebrows rose. "Whatever?" He continued to cross the room with slow, deliberate steps.

She knew she should hold her ground, knew she shouldn't let him see that he intimidated her. Still, she retreated. One step, then another and another, as he came closer.

Before Desiree knew it, she was backed against the kitchen counter, Jesse's long, lithe body only inches from her own. He smelled like horses, like fire, like sweat—a combination that should have been unpleasant but wasn't. She took a deep breath, savoring the sexy, seductive scent of him.

Electricity crackled between them. She wanted to touch him, to run her fingers through the silky darkness of his hair as she pressed her body to his and begged him to take her. She wanted to feel his lips on her, needed to touch and taste him everywhere at once. Her nipples peaked beneath her lace bra at the thought, and an ache started low in her belly as her breathing grew ragged. She watched his eyes darken to ebony, felt the heat radiating from him and knew, finally, that he wasn't nearly as unmoved as he wanted her to believe.

"Jesse." She was restless, aching for him in every cell of her being.

She watched his gaze drop to her breasts, felt his sudden intake of breath as he stared at the tight buds pressing against the thin silk of her dress. He leaned closer, crowding her, his chest scant inches from her own as his lips hovered over hers.

"Jesse." It was a plea, and both of them knew it. Her eyelids fluttered as seconds stretched into a minute. Then he was reaching for her, past her, snatching a carrot slice from the salad and turning away.

"I need to take a shower before we eat," he commented as he headed toward his bedroom, his breathing level and his long stride relaxed. "I'll make it quick."

Desiree stared, openmouthed, as the door closed behind him. Her knees trembled, but she locked them in place as fury ripped through her. The bastard. The unbelievable, arrogant bastard!

How dare he get her all stirred up, then walk away?

How dare he get that close, then not follow through?

How dare he not want her?

Her eyes narrowed as she heard the shower start, as she imagined him stripping that beautiful body. A picture rose in her head—him wet and naked, his long hair slicked back and his bronze body glistening as water and steam surrounded him.

Desire rose sharply and nearly drowned out the anger. Nearly.

Eyes narrowed in calculation, she drained the pasta, switched off the sauce. Should she have dinner ready and waiting when he got out, as if he hadn't just rejected her for the millionth time? Should she leave, duck out before he finished his shower? Everything in her—from her pride to her love for him—rebelled at the thought of turning tail. Or should she stay and seduce him as he'd never been seduced before?

Desiree grinned slyly—as if she even had to think about the choices. There was only one place she wanted to be and that was in the shower with him. She reviewed her earlier plan, making changes in her head even as she stealthily opened the bedroom door. She'd show Jesse. She'd make him beg to have her, make him grovel before he laid a hand on her.

Crossing the room to the open bathroom door, she inhaled his scent floating on the billowing steam. Watched as his silhouette moved behind the shower curtain. And began to undress. Quickly, before she second-guessed herself. Before she changed her mind.

When she was naked, Desiree took a deep breath and prayed that she was doing the right thing. Then, with fingers crossed, she slipped soundlessly into the shower.

Jesse faced the spray, his head bent as water cascaded over his hair and down his muscular chest. His arms were braced against the wall, the muscles in his arms and shoulders rigid.

He spun to face her as she closed the shower curtain and she nearly swallowed her tongue at her first look at his naked, heavily aroused body—so long and hard that she was sure he must be in pain. Any plans she had flew right out of her head.

"What are you doing?" he barked, his voice low and tormented as he stared at her.

She cleared her throat and moved so that she was next to him, so close she could share the warm spray. He tensed even more, shifting so she had more space. Though it was one of the hardest things she'd ever done, Desiree smiled and reached, with studied casualness, for a bottle of shampoo. "It occurred to me that I could use a shower, too. I've been working with the horses most of the day."

Of course, she'd spent nearly half an hour in her own shower—shaving and cleansing and moisturizing—before heading to Jesse's, but she saw no reason to bring that up. Tilting her head back, Desiree let the water wash over her short crop of red hair, lifting her hands to her head to lather in the shampoo, desperately aware of how her breasts lifted at the movement, her nipples puckering and begging for his attention.

She closed her eyes, but could still feel his hot gaze over her as his breathing grew harsh. Please, God, don't let him send her away. Don't let him reject her again.

"Desiree, stop." So low they were almost a growl, the words slammed into her, making her heart stutter and her body jerk.

She opened her eyes, stared into his, shocked at the anger and desire moving in them. She wanted to say something sophisticated, something sexy, but when she spoke, only the truth came out. "I can't."

She reached for him, but he grabbed her shoulders, kept her at arm's length. "We can't do this."

"Why can't we?" Her eyes wandered down to the proof of his desire. "I know you want me, and it's more than obvious that I want you. So what's the problem?" She clutched one of his hands in her own and pressed it to her breast.

Jesse groaned, his thumb sweeping over her hardened nipple of its own volition. For long moments he caressed her. He closed his eyes, a look of agony on his face as he moved to pull his hand away.

She grabbed it, held his fingers in place as she arched toward him. "Don't leave me like this, Jesse. Please, don't leave me."

Shuddering, he pulled her into the shelter of his body. He pressed his face into her neck as he fought for control. "I'm years too old for you, Desiree. I knew you when you were still a child."

Smiling, she reached down and let her fingers lightly travel the length of him. "I haven't been a child since the day I first saw you." She continued to stroke him, watched as his eyes grew hazy, listened as his breath hitched first once and then again. "And I'm certainly not a child now."

"I work for your father." The words were wrenched from him as he thrust helplessly against her hand.

"He's not here." She wrapped her arms around his neck and pressed her body fully against him. "This isn't about him." Leaning forward, she licked a drop of water from his chest—following the trail from his nipple to his throat to a spot right under his left ear.

"Desiree." Her name was ripped from him as he exploded, lifting her against the cool tile wall. His mouth captured hers, his tongue thrusting inside as he tasted every part of her. She moaned, her lips parting to give him better access as he devoured her.

His teeth closed over her lower lip, nipping at its fullness as he rolled her nipples between his thumbs and forefingers, pinching slightly, laughing as she gasped and arched against him.

She'd expected her first time to be slow and gentle, full of whispers and soft caresses. She'd dreamed of giving herself to Jesse, dreamed of sweetness and tenderness. What she got was none of that, yet somehow so much more.

His mouth raced frantically across her cheek, over her neck, down her breast until he reached her nipple. Pulling the hard nub into his mouth, he sucked, his tongue circling the areole. She gasped, moaned, pushed herself against his mouth as tension wound tighter and tighter within her.

He moved between her thighs, spreading her legs wide as his mouth continued to pull on her breast, his thumb slipping between them to find her hottest point.

Heat. Joy. Pleasure so intense she nearly convulsed swept through Desiree before she was ready, before she could prepare herself. She screamed, wrapping her legs around Jesse's waist, opening herself to him as he slid home.

Pain exploded inside of her and she tensed. She heard Jesse curse, felt his instinctive withdrawal. But the pain was fading quickly, a hot urgency taking its place so that she began moving frantically against him.

He groaned, low and deep, thrusting against her as his mouth moved once again to her own. She could tell he wanted to slow down, wanted to be gentle, but she was desperate for completion. Her body was spiraling up, up, beyond her control, and she wanted, needed to take him with her this first time.

She reached between them, rubbed her fingers over his peaked nipples, reveling in the groan he couldn't hold back.

"Stop!" he gasped. "It's too soon. You're not ready."

But she was ready, so ready that it was all she could do to keep from going off like a firecracker on the Fourth of July. And then his hand was between her legs, rubbing her and she couldn't hold back, didn't know how to hold back.

She screamed as her body convulsed, long and high and keening as Jesse slammed into her again and again. Suddenly he stiffened and pleasure like she'd never imagined swept through her, into her, holding her in its grasp for one long, timeless moment.

She didn't know how long they stayed like that—

a tangle of arms and legs and bodies pressing against the shower wall. But the water had run cold before the tremors shaking her subsided and he finally moved. She protested when he pulled away and let her legs slide down his slippery body until her feet hit the floor.

"Jesse—"

"Shh," he interrupted as he began to wash her quickly, skimming the washcloth intimately over her body before rinsing her off.

She willed him to say something, anything, willed him to gather her against him and hold on tight. But he was silent as he washed himself even more quickly before turning off the water.

She tried to talk to him once more, but he pinned her with a look of such anger and disgust that she shrank from him. He draped a towel around his hips, wrapped one around her and carried her into the bedroom, where he settled her gently on the bed.

Silence, tense and angry, stretched between them, and each minute that passed stretched her nerves a little bit tighter. Desiree watched as Jesse paced the room, his big hands raking through his hair again and again.

Finally, when she was nearly insane from the waiting, he sat on the bed near to her. His face was grim. "Why didn't you tell me?"

Confusion filled her. "Tell you what?"

"Don't play games with me, Desiree!" His voice

snapped with repressed rage. "You were a virgin. Why the hell didn't you mention that fact before…" He broke off.

"Before what?" Her temper flared before she could control it. "Before you made love to me? I didn't think it was important. And I figured you knew."

He stared at her in disbelief. "How the hell was I supposed to know? You sure didn't act like a virgin— coming here to sleep with me, climbing into the shower with me, touching me the way you did!" His voice rose with every word, until he was shouting.

Embarrassment swept through her at his reminder of her uninhibited behavior, but she'd be damned before she let him see it. "Who exactly am I supposed to have slept with? I've loved you since I was sixteen years old! Who else would I let touch me?"

His face darkened dangerously, frustration in every line of his body as he turned away, resting his elbows on his knees. She watched him breathe deeply—once, twice and then again and again—until the darkness slowly faded away and he turned back to her. "Desiree…"

She looked into his eyes, saw the regret he didn't even try to hide. She struggled to smile despite the pain of his rejection. She wanted to leave, wanted to be anywhere but here, doing anything but having this dis-cussion. Not now, while her body still hummed from her first orgasm. Not while her muscles ached pleasantly and all she really wanted to do was climb into the center of the bed with Jesse and make love again.

"You don't have to say anything," she said quietly, even as her heart broke. "I understand." She stood, pulling the towel more tightly around her as she squared her shoulders and looked him in the eye. "But I'm glad you didn't know. If it would have stopped you from making love to me, then I'm glad I didn't tell you."

"Is that what you think?" His eyes narrowed as he grabbed her hand, pulling her onto the bed beside him. "That I wouldn't have made love to you?" He sighed, his eyes steady and sincere on hers.

"Oh, darlin', you couldn't be more wrong." Jesse pulled her into his arms, let his lips trail lightly down her cheek. "I've wanted you since you were seventeen, Desiree. Years too young for me and so beautiful you broke my heart. There's no way I could have turned you away tonight, even though I wanted to. No way I could resist taking what I've wanted for five long years."

"Then why are you so angry at me?"

His smile was sad as his thumb brushed gently over her mouth. "Not you, darlin'. Never you." He gripped her hands in his, lowered his forehead until it rested on hers. "I'm angry with me. I shouldn't have taken you like that—fast and hard, up against a wall."

He shook his head, his mouth twisted with disgust.

"I hurt you and I didn't have to. If I'd known, if I hadn't been so blind, I'd have done it differently. I'd still have loved you—I don't think anything could have stopped me after all these years of needing you— but I would have made damn sure it was good for you."

Tears flooded her eyes before she could stop them as all her dreams came true at once. "It was good for me, Jesse. Wonderful. Fantastic. Amazing." She leaned into his warmth, savoring the feel of his nakedness against her.

Pulling her into his lap, he ran his hands through her hair as he cuddled her against him. Desiree relaxed slowly as she listened to the strong, steady beat of his heart. "I love you."

"I know, darlin'." His voice was heavy, his eyes sad and dark. "God knows you shouldn't, but I'm so glad you do." He brushed his lips against hers.

It was supposed to be a soft kiss, a safe kiss, but she lit up at the first touch of his mouth. Pulling him tightly against her, Desiree slowly traced his lips with her tongue before pulling his bottom lip between her teeth. She nipped playfully, laughed as he groaned against her, as he pushed her gently onto the bed and covered her body with his own.

"Are you sore?" he asked, sliding his knee between her own.

Her smile blazed as she wrapped her arms around his neck. "Not even a little."

"Then why don't I do this right this time?" He leaned down, traced the hollow of her neck with his tongue.

She shivered, arching up to give him better access. "I didn't think there was anything wrong with last time, but practice…mmm…makes perfect."

He grinned as he lowered his mouth to her nipple. "Desiree?"

"Yes?" Her voice was low, breathless.

"You do know that I'm a perfectionist, don't you?"

She shuddered as his fingers found her and began to stroke. "Thank goodness."

CHAPTER SEVEN

JESSE BENT TO PICK up the shards of glass from the tumbler he'd thrown earlier, grimacing when one of the pieces sliced his finger. The glass had been one of a set her father had prized—given to him by the last man who'd ever trained a horse that won the Triple Crown, Big John had sworn the glasses were lucky.

So much for luck. Still, Jesse shouldn't have thrown the stupid thing—the glasses were a tangible symbol of everything Desiree wanted and therefore were special to her. Besides, it didn't belong to him. Like everything else on this ranch, it belonged to Desiree and would be passed on to their children when she died.

The fact that she came from money didn't bother him—through the years he'd made a lot of money himself through his share of the winners' purses as well as his hefty salary. Enough to start Cherokee Dreaming. Money wasn't, and had never been, the issue.

What bothered him, what had always bothered him, was the fact that he and Desiree didn't have a place of their own. A place that he had contributed to as much as, if not more than she had.

He threw away the pieces then crossed to the frame he'd knocked off the wall in his earlier fury. Without looking at the picture, he piled the broken glass on it before carrying it across the study to the trash can. It was only after he'd discarded the glass that he realized which frame had fallen.

It was then that he began to shake, even as he tried to ignore the yellowed newspaper article. Even as he told himself to remount it, to leave it on the desk, to walk away, he found himself reading the words Desiree had saved so long ago, and for a brief moment he was thrust back to where so much of this had begun.

And in horseracing news, Desiree Hawthorne, 23, only child of renowned Thoroughbred rancher and racer Big John Hawthorne, has wed Jesse Rainwater, 38, a man considered by many to be the best trainer in the business.

The two were wed in a quiet ceremony in Las Vegas and are currently honeymooning in Hawaii. The ceremony was attended by only two witnesses, as the bride's father was not in attendance and the groom's parents are deceased.

In a statement released earlier today, the bride writes, "Jesse and I are thrilled to celebrate our love through the lifelong commitment of marriage. After the honeymoon, we will be settling on the Triple H, where we will concentrate on upholding the legacy of one of the best and brightest Thoroughbred ranches in America."

"ARE YOU SURE you want to do this?" Jesse asked, as he opened the hotel room door.

"I'm positive." Desiree's voice was firm as she preceded him into the room, but he saw her chin wobble a little as she spoke.

Dropping the bags, Jesse kicked the door shut with one booted foot before gathering her into his arms. His lips skimmed over her hair, down her cheek and he spent a moment, just a moment, reveling in the wildflower and honey scent of her. For the first time in memory she was stiff in his arms, her firm, rounded curves unyielding against him.

Her unusual reticence made him nervous. Pulling away, he said, "I mean it, Desiree. If you're having second thoughts, we can forget about it. We can stay a couple of nights, have some fun, do a little gambling then head home—a minivacation."

"Me?" She laughed, the sound more sad than joyous. "This whole thing was my idea. Why would I be the one to back out now that we're here?"

He shrugged, going to the window to look out at the bright lights and milling people that made up so much of the Las Vegas strip. "You've been nervous since we got off the plane. I thought reality might have suddenly set in, that's all."

"What exactly does that mean?"

He turned at the sharpness of her tone, one eyebrow raised. "You're not acting like the woman who proposed to me eight days ago or even like the one who got on the plane with me this morning. I'm wondering if maybe you think this is a bad idea."

"Me? It took everything I had just to get you to the airport this morning." Her arms were crossed defensively over her chest, and her lower lip stuck out in a definite pout. It was a look he'd never seen on her before and one he couldn't help being a little bit aroused by.

"I'm here, aren't I? And you're the one who's suddenly acting nervous." He studied her, watched anger flicker in her slumberous eyes.

"That's your big concession? That you're here? Well, don't I feel special now?" Picking up her suitcase, she hurled it onto the bed and began unpacking with stiff, uncoordinated movements.

"You know, you could just tell me what's wrong instead of going through this asinine, juvenile game."

He caught the hairbrush that came hurtling at him just before it collided with his eye. "I am not juvenile!" she yelled, even as she looked for something else to launch.

"I didn't say you were." He ducked in time to

miss a flying red stiletto. "But then again, you are the one having the temper tantrum."

She screamed, before chucking her makeup bag, a bottle of her favorite perfume and her hair dryer at him in quick succession. He ducked under the first, caught the second, but wasn't fast enough to keep the third from banging painfully against his hip.

"What the hell is wrong with you?" he roared indignantly. "If you don't want to get married, then just say so!"

"I'm not the one who doesn't want to get married, Rainwater." Her voice rose with each word until he was certain that half the hotel could hear her. "Admit it. You think this is a horrible idea."

Her chest heaved with each word. Fire was in her eyes, rage in the fists clenched on her hips, and she'd never been more beautiful to him than she was right then. Lost, he stared at her, hoping to find some clue on how to negotiate the suddenly rocky sea of their relationship.

She stared at him for a long time, waiting for an answer he couldn't give. When it finally became apparent to her that he wasn't going to say anything, she sank to the floor. With her back resting against the bed and her arms wrapped around herself, she stared straight ahead and silently rocked herself.

"Desiree." He knelt beside her and tried to gather her in his arms, but she wouldn't allow him to comfort her.

"It's okay," she said, her voice uncharacteristically subdued as she faced him. "It's completely my fault. This was a stupid idea, totally ridiculous." Her smile was grim, her laugh painful to hear. "It's not your fault that you don't love me."

Shock raced through him, holding him immobile as precious seconds ticked by. By the time he regained his voice, he got the feeling that it was too little, too late. "Of course I love you. How could you doubt that?"

"You're a terrible liar, Jess. Unconvincing and extremely slow on the uptake." She tried to smile, but her lips remained curved downward. "It's okay. I thought I could love you enough for both of us."

"I *do* love you."

She shook her head, then pushed to her feet and began picking up the things she'd thrown in her earlier rage. As if she'd already given up on him—on them.

"Stop it." His voice was low, rusty with the panic skating over every one of his nerves.

When she didn't look up or even acknowledge that she'd heard him, he crossed the room in a couple of long strides. Ignoring her squeal of protest, he scooped her up and tossed her onto the empty side of the lake-size bed. Before she could move or even protest, he'd climbed on top of her and straddled her hips with his legs.

She squirmed beneath him, tried to wiggle away.

He caught his breath sharply as she rubbed repeatedly against him, his body responding predictably to her movements. He could tell by her sudden stillness, by the wariness in her eyes, that she had felt his response.

"This isn't going to solve anything," she said, her eyes widening as he lowered his mouth to hers.

"I think it'll solve everything," he replied right before he claimed her mouth with his own.

She felt amazing, had felt amazing from the very first time he had held her in his arms. How could she think he didn't love her? He would die for her.

With a moan of surrender, she returned the kiss. The hands that had been pushing on his chest slid upward to his neck, anchoring him in place as she wrapped her suddenly pliant body around him.

He wanted to lose himself in the sweet, seductive haven of her arms. But he pulled away even as she whimpered, ended the kiss even as she opened herself to him.

She closed her eyes, turning her head away before he could speak.

"No, not this time." He grasped her chin with gentle fingers, turning her face until he could look her in the eye. "This time we finish this."

Rolling off her, he pulled her into his arms, his cheek resting on the top of her head. "How could you think that I don't love you?"

She sighed. "Jesse…"

"No, I'm serious. How on earth could you not realize that you mean everything to me?" He clutched her hands in his own, pulling away slightly so that she could see what he felt for her. "Desiree, I love you more than my own life. I always have."

Her eyes widened, but he could still see the suspicion. "You never said—"

Sighing, he allowed his forehead to drop until it rested against hers. "I know."

"Not once." Her voice was choked. "You never said you loved me. You never came after me. You never did any of the things a man in love does." She pushed against him, her eyes bright with anger, fear and a burgeoning hope that was almost painful to see.

"*I* had to chase *you*. I had to *strip naked and seduce you* before you would even touch me. I was the one who asked you to marry me. I was the one who did *everything*."

"I'm so sorry. I wanted to buy you flowers and take you nice places. I wanted to be the one who took care of you, who proposed to you. But I was too damn uncertain, too damn scared to do it."

"What did you possibly have to be scared of? I was the one risking everything, Jesse. I was the one who dealt with rejection after rejection. Even when I asked you to marry me, you sighed and said, 'I guess so.' Who does that?"

"I didn't want to mess up your life."

"Bull—"

"No, you asked. Now you'll listen." He rolled away from her, stared up at the ceiling as he searched within himself for the words.

"I'm a half-breed Indian whose only talent in life is in dealing with horses. I come from nowhere, and before I found the Triple H, I was going nowhere fast."

"That's ridiculous. You're one of the most talented trainers in the country, Jesse. Everyone knows that— your future is as bright as you want it to be."

"I'm the hired help, Desiree. I'm not like you. I don't have a big, fancy horse-breeding pedigree behind me. I don't have a fancy education or a guaranteed place in the horse-racing community." He paused, raised his hands so that she could see the nicks and calluses that were so much a part of who he was and what he did. "Look at me. I'm making good money now—I can support you—but it's not the same. I'm not as rich as your father or as fancy as all those men he's spent the past year introducing you to."

He rolled over, stared into her endless blue eyes. "I don't want you to regret marrying me in a few years, or a few months, when your blinders come off and you see what everyone else does—the half-breed scrambling to make something of himself."

Desiree shoved him away from her. "Don't say that. Don't you ever say that."

Her cheeks were red, her eyes blazing with indignation. "I love you, Jesse. The real you, not some man you think I've romanticized in my head. You are so much more than you think you are. You're smart and brave and so incredibly talented that you awe me."

She reached out, ran a hand through his hair. "God knows you're not perfect, but I love you. I love you and I want to build my life with you. I don't know how else to say it."

He closed his eyes, thanked God for this most beautiful, most amazing woman that he had been gifted with. "Then let's go get married, darlin'."

Her smile, when it came, was brilliant. "Are you sure?"

He laughed, nuzzling her cheek with his lips. "Hell, no. I figure your father will kick us off the ranch as soon as he sees your wedding ring."

"He'll get over it," she answered confidently as she ran her fingers lightly over the nape of his neck.

"Maybe in twenty years or so."

She laughed. "More like twenty minutes or so. Daddy is nothing if not pragmatic. If he disowns me, who's going to run the ranch when he's gone?"

"I think he'll be less than impressed with the idea of you running it while married to a half-Indian horse-trainer with a lousy pedigree."

"Oh, I don't know." She smiled mischievously. "You bring home the Triple Crown and all will be forgiven."

"We'll see about that."

She flipped him over so that she was straddling him, her soft lower body rocking gently against his suddenly hard one. "You did remind me of something else we need to take care of though."

He arched up, reveling in the little hitch of her breath as he did so. Reaching up, he caressed her breasts through the thin silk of her blouse. "What's that, darlin'?"

Moaning as his hands found her tight nipples, Desiree let her head loll back as she moved restlessly against him. "Wedding rings," she gasped, arching into the rhythmic stroking of his fingers.

He paused as her words sunk in, his mouth mere inches from her breast. Moaning her disappointment, she thrust herself against him even as he moved to lift her off him.

"What are you doing?" she demanded, her fingers moving swiftly over the buttons of her blouse.

"Getting your ring."

"I didn't mean now," she pouted. "Come back to bed and finish what you started. We can go shopping later."

Rummaging in his overnight bag, he tossed her a grin over his shoulder. "I don't have to go shopping. I bought this for you two months ago."

"Two months ago?" Sitting up quickly, her open blouse forgotten, she stared at him incredulously. "I just proposed to you eight days ago."

"I know." Returning swiftly, he crouched between

her open legs and handed her a small, red box. "I've been carrying it around for weeks, trying to come up with the right way to ask you."

She stared at him with her mouth half-open, completely dumbfounded. "You were going to propose to me?" she asked.

"Well, yeah. That's what a man does when he finds the woman he wants to spend the rest of his life with."

"But you sounded so unenthusiastic when I asked you that I nearly died."

"I said yes, didn't I?"

"Barely."

"You caught me off guard." He pushed a lock of hair away from his eyes so that he could see her clearly. "I didn't have the ring on me, I hadn't made any plans and there you were, jumping the gun on me—as usual. I wasn't ready."

"I couldn't wait any longer."

"I think that's the nicest thing you've ever said to me." He nodded at the box in her hands. "Are you going to open that or simply stare at it all day?"

With a nervous smile, she flipped the lid open and gasped, one hand flying to her mouth as she stared at the engagement ring he had picked out after much deliberation. The center stone was huge—a two-carat, almost flawless solitaire—while the band was lined all the way around with smaller, channel-set diamonds.

"Do you like it?" he asked, more nervous than he

liked to admit. He'd searched for days for the perfect ring and had fallen in love with this one the second he laid eyes on it. Elegant but fun, it seemed to fit both sides of Desiree's personality.

"It's the most beautiful thing I've ever seen." She started to take it from the box, but he stopped her.

"Allow me." Grasping her suddenly shaking hand in his steady one, Jesse kissed her open palm lingeringly. As he slid the ring home, he murmured, "I'm going to make you happy, Desiree. I swear it."

She cupped his face in her hands, the diamond on her finger gleaming brightly in the Las Vegas sunshine. "You already do."

Smiling, she pulled him onto the bed with her, her eyes gleaming seductively as she slid her fingers inside the waistband of his jeans. "But I know how I can be happier."

He tugged off his T-shirt in one smooth, coordinated move before slowly sliding her blouse off her shoulders. "Give me a couple of minutes and I'll make you ecstatic."

"I'm counting on it," she murmured as she slowly stretched out over the brightly colored bedspread.

"Me, too, darlin'. Me, too."

CHAPTER EIGHT

THIS WAS BETRAYAL. Desiree stared at the letter Rio had just handed her. She read it a second time, then a third, as she struggled to assimilate what it said. Struggled to deal with the fact that her husband and oldest son had conspired behind her back.

Everything inside her demanded that she attack, but she did her best to ignore the impulse. They might have blindsided her with this, but she refused to go off half-cocked and emotional.

"Mom." Rio's voice was low, pleading. "This is all I've ever wanted to be."

"A veterinarian?" she demanded. She hadn't fought as hard as she had to continue the ranch's tradition only to have her son walk away from everything she wanted to give him. Shaking the letter for emphasis, she strode across the stable toward him. "You want to go all the way to Colorado State so that you can be a veterinarian?"

"It's the best program in the country," Jesse said

as he put a hand on his eighteen-year-old son's shoulder. "One of the top in the world."

"It's almost impossible to get into, Mom. But I did it. I made it and I want to go."

"Why am I just now hearing about this? We sat down, the three of us, months ago and talked about your future. We talked about where you were going to apply and what you were going to major in. At no time did you bring up Colorado State or veterinary school. I would remember if you had."

Rio looked at his father pleadingly. "Dad and I—"

"Oh? You did this behind my back?" she asked Jesse.

He cocked his head, stared at her with unfathomable eyes. "We didn't want to upset you until we knew if Rio could actually get into a preveterinary program."

"So you knew I'd be upset? Yet you did it anyway?" She paced away, her hands clenched angrily at her side. "What is wrong with you?" She whirled to face her son. "Your job is supposed to be this ranch, Rio. You're supposed to go to school and study business so that you're ready to run the Triple H when something happens to me." God, what would she do if Rio wasn't there to assume control? Would that be yet another way she failed to meet her father's expectations?

"I know that, Mom."

"Then what's all this talk of being a veterinarian?"

"Desi—"

"Don't you Desi me, Jesse. I'm not even talking

to you right now. You deliberately did this behind my back. You deliberately kept your mouth shut and let me think that everything was going the way it was supposed to."

"Supposed to?" The words burst from Rio. "Nothing is ever like it's supposed to be around here, Mom!"

"What does that mean?" she asked.

"It means that I don't want the ranch! I've never wanted it. Only, you've never been able to see that."

The words hung in the air, a land mine waiting to detonate with one wrong move. Minutes ticked by as Desiree stared at her son in silence. When she finally spoke, her voice was ice-cold. "What makes you think you have a choice in the matter? The oldest child has inherited this ranch for the last four generations, Rio. My great-grandfather, my grandfather, my father, me. Do you think this is what all of us wanted to do with our lives?" Opening her arms wide, she gestured to the stable and beyond. "Do you think I wanted to spend my life chasing an award that we seem absolutely incapable of winning? Do you think I wanted to spend my life tied up with horses and ledgers and breeding charts?"

"If you hate it so much, why are you trying to make me do it?" His voice sounded young, and it was clear from the expression on his face that Rio hated it.

"Because it is your responsibility." Her voice cut like a knife. "It is your legacy and I will not let you turn your back on it."

"He's not turning his back on anything, Desiree. Why can't he be a veterinarian and still take over the ranch when you retire?"

"Because that's not what he wants," she said. "He wants to run away from here, wants to completely forget any responsibility he has to this place." Her laugh was harsh. "He plans on turning his back on everything he's been trained for, everything five generations of my family have worked for. Even better, he wants me to pay for him while he does it."

"No, Mom, it's not like that. Dad—"

"Oh, so your dad's going to pay for your education? For your defection?" Her gaze cut to her husband. "Of course, all his money came from the Triple H, too. Hasn't it, Jess? All your wealth and fame has come directly from this ranch, even though you've never done the one thing I've asked of you, the one thing my father asked of you."

Jesse blanched. "Go up to the house, Rio."

"But—"

"Go!" he commanded sharply, as he stalked across the stable toward his wife.

Rio took off running without another word, his feet flying over the gravel and grass between the stables and the house. Jesse watched his son go, waited until he had vanished from sight before turning toward Desiree.

"Who the hell do you think you are?" he asked.

"I know exactly who I am. I am your wife, his

mother and the owner of this ranch. As such, I deserve some input into how he spends the rest of his life."

"He isn't one of your employees." Jesse bit out the words from between clenched teeth. "You can't order him around and make him do what you want with the rest of his life."

"This ranch—"

"Screw the ranch, Desiree. Open your eyes and look at your son. How could you not know this was coming? How could you be so goddamn shocked?"

He grabbed her, shook her. "He's been bringing home wounded animals since he was five—birds, dogs, cats, even mice, for God's sake. He's read book after book on animals and with each wounded stray he's gotten better at fixing them up. He shadows Paul and Devon whenever they show up here, asking question after question about what they're doing and why and how they're doing it. Did you think it was just idle curiosity?"

"I…" She broke off, stared at her husband in bewilderment.

His eyes widened with sudden understanding. "You never even noticed. You're so wrapped up in this ranch that you don't even see your own children anymore."

"That's not true." But she had the sinking feeling it was.

"Isn't it?" He thrust her away. "Did you see his face when you made that reference to the Triple

Crown, to the promise I haven't been able to keep? Have you ever taken the time to look at them, at what your obsession is doing to this family?"

"It's not an obsession. This ranch—"

"Is a piece of property, Desiree. It's land and horses. Beautiful land, beautiful horses, yes, but still just property. But Rio—he's so much more than that."

Fury consumed her. "I don't need you to tell me about my son!"

"*Our* son. Rio's my son, too. And yeah, I do think you need someone to tell you about him, about all of our children because sometimes I wonder if they even register on your radar anymore."

"That's a horrible thing to say. I love my children and I want what's best for them."

He shook his head. "Who are you trying to kid, Desiree? You want what you've always wanted— you want what's best for this ranch. If our children's needs and desires happen to coincide, then everything's fine. But if they want something different, if they need something away from this albatross, then all hell breaks loose."

"I've always put my children first."

He laughed, but there was no humor in the sound. "So why are we even having this discussion? If you always put your children first, why is it even an issue that Rio wants to be a veterinarian?"

Her eyes narrowed. "That's different."

"Why? Because you want it to be?"

"He's throwing away his whole life!"

He stared at her incredulously. "Training to be a vet is ruining his life? Doing what he loves, what he's always loved? He's going to college, Desiree, not running drugs or knocking over convenience stores."

"You don't understand!"

"You're damn right I don't. What's there to understand? Rio wants to do something other than run this ranch—so what? You've got two other kids who love the ranch, not to mention the fact that you're not close to handing over the reins, for God's sake. A lot can happen in twenty-five years. Rio can, and probably will, change his mind about the ranch. Dakota or Willow may really want to take over, or the whole operation may end up bankrupt. You never know, so why are we even arguing about this right now?"

"I had plans—"

"And you're the only one? I have plans, Rio has plans, everyone has plans. Plans that have nothing to do with this ranch or the stupid Triple Crown." He shook his head. "What's happened to you?"

"Nothing."

He continued as if he hadn't heard her protest. "I look at you and I see the young girl I fell in love with, the girl with the intense eyes that could see all the way to my soul. The girl who could see every part of me with just a look."

He reached a restless hand out to pat Will-o-the-Wisp, who was nickering softly, nervously. "God, you were amazing. So full of fire and life that I couldn't help wanting you, needing you. You were wild and reckless and impulsive—everything that I wasn't. Being with you was like having a comet by the tail—it was impossible to do anything but hang on and hope to survive the ride."

"Nobody can live their life with that kind of intensity all the time, Jess. It isn't practical." Her voice was subdued.

"I know that. But it would be nice to see glimpses of that girl every once in a while. The girl who snuck out of the house to sit with the sick horses in the middle of the night, who worked in a soup kitchen even though her father forbade it." He smiled. "The girl who drove me crazy with her sultry looks and sexy perfume, who seduced me, who made me love her despite all the warnings I gave myself."

"I'm the same woman I've always been."

He shook his head, stared at her with a sadness and an intensity that had her breath catching in her throat. "The woman who dragged me to Vegas against her father's will would understand a child's need to live his or her own life, despite parental wishes."

He raked a hand through his hair. "The ranch means everything to you. We know that. But you can't expect everyone to feel about it the same way you do."

Desiree walked to her office, stared at the pictures of her children on the corner of her desk. When she turned to face Jesse, tears threatened. "I just want what's best for him."

"He's eighteen, darlin'. It's time to let him decide what that is."

"What if he's wrong?"

"What if he's not?" His mouth twisted wryly. "You can't keep them wrapped in cotton forever. No matter how much you want to keep them safe."

She reached for her husband's hand despite the hints of betrayal still zinging through her system. "I know about the animals, Jess. All the wounded animals and people Rio's brought home through the years and tried to help. Just as I've seen him break his heart over the ones he couldn't help. I've seen the pain and helplessness he feels when he's done everything he can and it still isn't enough." Her thumb rubbed circles on Jesse's hand. "I don't want a lifetime of that kind of pain for him. Is that so bad?"

"Helping isn't a job to Rio, darlin'. It's a vocation. And he'll be doing it for the rest of his life, whether he becomes a vet or not."

She sighed, cuddled against his side. "That doesn't mean I have to like it."

"No. But it does mean you can't bitch about it for the next fifteen years."

She laughed before she could stop herself. Jesse

looked startled, but then joined in as he drew her closer to him. Minutes passed silently as they held on to each other before Desiree finally pulled away.

"Jesse?" Her voice was tentative, nervous.

"What's wrong, Desiree?"

"I know you gave up a lot to marry me. I know that you never planned on spending thirty years chasing an unattainable dream."

He sighed. "That's not what I meant."

"I know. But it's true, nonetheless. If you've got something you have to do, some dream you haven't realized, then I want you to do it."

"Desiree—"

"No," she shook her head adamantly. "I don't want to be the one who cost you your dreams. So whatever it is that you can't get from me, from the Triple H, I want you to go after it."

He shook his head. "It's not practical, Desiree."

"Since when are dreams practical, Jesse? Just promise me you'll always come back. Promise me you'll never leave me."

"Where would I go, darlin'? You and our children are my life."

"Maybe it's time you had a little more than that."

"There is nothing more than that."

"Not more, then. Just different. Whatever it is, I'll support you, Jess. And I'll support Rio, though I don't understand why he can't go to A & M. They've got a great veterinary program and they're so much closer than Colorado State."

He smiled, rocked her softly. "You've got to let them go sometime, darlin'."

"And we both know how good I am at letting go of the things and people I love."

"It'll get easier."

"If it doesn't kill me."

CHAPTER NINE

THE STUDY DOOR SLAMMED open for the second time that day, and Jesse turned to see Desiree all but breathing fire as she glared at him. Her flame-red hair was a mess—as if she'd spent the past few hours yanking at it. Her full mouth was set in a grim line and her expression dared him to speak before she'd had her say.

He expected her to yell, to let loose the redheaded temper she usually kept under such stringent control. But when she spoke, her voice was low and her teeth clenched as she spat out each word. Somehow her control made the words even more effective.

"I don't have a clue what's going on in your head and haven't for a hell of a long time. But until those papers are signed, until they are certified by a judge, I am still your wife. And I do not appreciate the disrespect you showed by walking away from me in the middle of our conversation."

He smirked, knowing how much it would annoy her. "I wouldn't exactly call that a conversation, darlin.' More like a haranguing and I didn't feel the need to hang around for it."

"Stop calling me that!"

Her shriek made him take a step back, had him looking warily at the numerous items the room provided for her to throw at him. Even so, a man had to stand his ground sometime—even if it meant getting beaned in the head with a paperweight. "Stop what?"

"Stop calling me darlin' in that sarcastic, condescending tone! You've been doing it all day, all month, all year. And I'm sick of it." Her voice escalated, threatening his hearing with every syllable.

"How dare you? How dare you hurt me by using the one and only endearment you've ever had for me to humiliate me now? How dare you spring this on me on the day of our daughter's wedding? How dare you tear apart our whole goddamn marriage and never give me a reason why!"

Crossing to the window, she wrapped her arms around her waist defensively.

He regarded her for a minute, unsure of what to say or do. Crossing the room before he could stop himself, he laid his hand on her shoulder before he thought better of it.

"Look, darlin', I'm sorry. Maybe I should have waited a couple of days to give you—"

She shrugged his hand away angrily. "I told you not to call me that."

Shock pulsed through him at the strange thickness in her voice, a thickness he hadn't heard in many years. "Are you crying?" He was so startled that the question slipped out before he could stop it.

"Of course not," she said bitterly. "Over you?"

Grabbing her shoulders roughly, he spun her to face him. "Don't be ridiculous, *darlin.'* I know better than to think—" He stopped abruptly as he stared at her wet cheeks, at her gorgeous blue eyes, wet and rimmed with red.

"Desiree?" His voice was quiet now, his touch tentative as he brushed the tears away with a few sweeps of his thumb. "I don't understand what's going on here."

"That makes two of us."

Uncertainty swept through him as he stared at the wife he thought he knew, and the tears he'd never expected. "Look, I'm not trying to hurt you."

Her chin came up. "As if you could."

"Then why are you crying?"

"Because I'm angry, you jerk. Because I was completely blindsided by your little announcement, and it's taking me some time to get used to it."

"Blindsided?" He gaped at her. "How the hell could you be blindsided? What have we done together in the past year? In the past two years?"

"The races—"

"Besides work. Besides the ranch. Besides the Triple Crown. What have we done together?"

"I thought you liked it that way."

"Liked living with you like a stranger or worse, like a boss and her employee? You thought I liked that?"

"You keep saying that." She stared at him with baffled eyes. "It's never been like that."

"It's always been like that, whether you admit it or not."

"How can you say that? After twenty-seven years, how can you say that to me?"

"How can I not?"

"You're insane. Completely nuts. I don't know what kind of sick thoughts you've got twisting around in that head of yours, but I won't be a part of it. I won't let you blame me for your own indifference."

"Indifference? Where the hell do you get that?"

She strode away from him. When she turned to face him, her chest heaved with exertion. Though he damned himself and his suddenly out-of-control libido, he couldn't tear his eyes from her. From her high, proud breasts that moved with every harsh breath to her flushed cheeks and burning eyes—she was magnificent and always had been. This woman he'd married who had always been too good for him.

"You throw divorce papers at me—you don't even tell me what they are—then you walk away like I'm nothing to you. Like we never raised a family together, like we never built this ranch together. Like we never even loved each other. What am I supposed to think, Jesse? It's been months since you moved out of our bedroom without so much as a word. Longer than that since you've held me or kissed me or made love to me. What the hell am I supposed to think?"

"You never said a word when I moved out!" The words burst from him defensively.

"What was I supposed to do? Beg you to touch me? To love me?"

"I wanted—"

"Someone else!"

Silence reigned as his heart stuttered in his chest, as he struggled to assimilate her words. She didn't believe…couldn't actually think…

"Is that what you think?" His voice was nearly un-recognizable when he finally spoke. "That I've been having an affair?"

"Don't you dare look so offended. What the hell else am I supposed to think? From the time we first got together you haven't been able to keep your hands off me, Jesse. And not just for sex, though we've had a hell of a lot of that, too. You've always responded to me, always touched me. Even if it was just a kiss or a hand on my cheek or the small of my back, you've always reached for me.

"When that stops as abruptly as it did with us, when you don't make love to me for over a year, when you don't even see me when I'm right in front of you, how can I think it's anything but another woman?"

"Do you even know me at all? Thirty-three years and you think that I'd betray you? For what?"

"I don't know!" She yelled at him. "All I know is you're gone and I don't know how to reach you. I know I'm getting older and I'm not as attractive—"

"Stop it." How could she think he didn't want her? "That's—"

But she was talking over him, through him. "You're away from home four and five months a year. I know beautiful, younger women throw themselves at you—I've seen it. And I know my stomach's not as flat as it used to be, that my breasts—"

"Desiree, don't—"

"Stop lying, Jesse. Stop—"

His mouth crushed hers punishingly, as rage and pain and fear swept through him. His hands tangled in her hair, pulled her head back roughly as he possessed her, devoured her.

She opened her mouth to protest and his tongue swept in—tasting, testing, teasing. Desiree moaned and the hands she'd brought up to push him away suddenly clutched his shirt, pulling him closer.

How could she think he didn't want her or that he would choose someone else before her? The questions taunted him as he devoured her, filling himself with the heady, seductive taste of her. He was desperate—a starving man too long denied the sustenance he needed most.

She tasted the same, like wildflowers and rain and the most exclusive dark chocolate. He craved her and had for a very long time. She was in his blood, in his heart, in his very soul. How had he thought to rid himself of her? How had he thought he could live without her?

Moaning, Desiree pressed herself against him and he forgot all the reasons this was a bad idea. He was caught up in feelings, mesmerized by the sensory explosion that had happened the second his mouth touched hers.

He opened his eyes, triumph roaring through him at the slight flush passion lent to her pale, milky-white skin—a familiar sight, yet new, as well. Everything felt new and exciting as he savored this unexpected happening, as he gloried in the feel of his wife—his *wife*—in his arms again. Finally.

She was beautiful. More beautiful now in her maturity than she'd been when he married her. Giving birth to his children had filled her out, rounding her body in all the right places. Her breasts were fuller, but still as high and firm as they'd been in her youth—testament to the exercises she performed religiously. Her legs—rider's legs—were long and lithe and her skin was incredibly soft to the touch. Her stomach was flat, and though her rear had filled out a little in the past few years, it looked good on her.

So where were her insecurities coming from?

Where had she gotten the idea that she was no longer attractive to him? Hell, of all the problems they had, sexual attraction had never been one of them. From the first moment he'd touched her he had burned for her—so hot and deep that twenty-seven years wasn't nearly enough time for the flame to flicker out.

Suddenly she pulled away, ending the connection as abruptly as he had begun it. "I have to go." She gestured to the door, as she tried to slip past him.

He stared at her blankly until she pushed at him a little. "Jesse, let me pass, please."

He nodded, turning slightly to allow her to exit as he struggled for control. He watched her walk to the door, watched her hand close convulsively on the handle. "Desiree."

He saw her stiffen, her body shuddering once, twice, before she regained control. Tension was a time bomb ticking inside of him as he contemplated the sorrow in Desiree's eyes before she'd moved past him, as he saw again the sad smile that didn't come close to reaching her eyes.

"I need to check on Willow." Her voice was subdued. "I have to make sure everything's going well with the florists, the caterers. I need—"

"Desiree."

Her eyes darted to his. "Not now, Jess. I can't do this now. We'll talk later. We'll… Later." She closed the door behind her.

He had his own duties to take care of for the wedding. So why was he still standing here? What had he expected? For one moment of passion to soften her? That the fleeting connection they'd experienced would last?

It never had before. Why should today be any different? From the moment she'd gained control of the ranch, Desiree had been out of his reach.

Shoulders slumped, head down—the pride of a lifetime battered if not completely vanquished—Jesse turned toward the wall of photos and ribbons and newspaper articles Desiree had obsessively saved for the past twenty years. With unerring accuracy, his gaze found the one that had almost single-handedly changed his life. The one that had sent Desiree into a tailspin and set him on a path he'd never planned on taking.

Horseracing legend and Triple H ranch owner Big John Hawthorne died today after suffering a massive heart attack. He was rushed to Breckenridge Hospital in Austin, Texas, after his son-in-law, Jesse Rainwater, found him collapsed inside one of the Triple H stables.

Though Hawthorne was born into horseracing royalty, he was never content to rest on the accomplishments of those who came before him. Considered a visionary by many in the business, he and the Triple H are responsible for many of the advances in Thoroughbred breeding and racing that have occurred in the past twenty-five years.

In recent years, his horses have won nearly every prestigious race the American horseracing world has to offer—except, ironically, the Triple Crown. Many in the horseracing community attribute his unparalleled success to a keen eye for horses and an even keener eye for personnel. Perhaps his biggest coup was landing the legendary Rainwater to train his horses, a stroke of genius that many believe is directly responsible for the recent fame and prestige of the Triple H.

Hawthorne is survived by his daughter Desiree Hawthorne-Rainwater, Rainwater and his three grandchildren Rio, Dakota and Willow Rainwater.

As dictated by family tradition, Hawthorne's only child, Hawthorne-Rainwater, will inherit the ranch her father poured so much of his heart and genius into. The question on the lips of nearly everyone involved in American horseracing this morning is how will she handle the responsibility? Can she live up to the high expectations set by her father or will she step aside and let Rainwater, her husband of nine years, run the ranch according to his own specifications?

Those closest to Hawthorne-Rainwater

believe that she has both the skill and the drive to take over for her father. "Desiree's been trained for this from the time she was a small child," comments Brian Willings, an official for the National Horseracing Association. "She is not only willing to take over for her father but also extremely capable and knowledgeable—perhaps even more than he was. Most of us in the business expect great things from Desiree and the Triple H. The next few years should prove extremely interesting."

Jesse watched closely as Desiree stripped off the black dress and stockings she'd worn to the funeral. He suddenly didn't know who this woman was— where was the Desiree that had raged when her mother died, the one who had cried in his arms?

This quiet, composed woman who wore duty like a shield wasn't his wife. He understood that she was in shock—Big John's heart attack had taken everyone by surprise. But Jesse had expected some kind of reaction, something that demonstrated how much their lives had changed overnight.

"Are you all right?" he asked, crossing the room to lay a warm hand on her shoulder.

"I'm fine." She shrugged off his support as she slipped a dark purple turtleneck over her head. "I've got a ton of things to do."

He stripped off his own jacket and tie. "The ranch can wait for a day or two, Desiree."

"Not really, Jesse." She was polite, remote, a totally different woman than he had held in his arms four days earlier…before her father had died. "There are decisions to be made, people to be contacted. It's our busiest season." She pulled on a pair of jeans, reached for her favorite boots.

"People understand, darlin'. Hell, just about everyone in the business was there today."

"They still expect the ranch to be run properly, Jess."

"They expect, and understand, that you'll need time to grieve for your father."

"What they expect is for me to fall flat on my face, and I'm not going to let that happen." Her eyes shot fire at him even as her lower lip trembled a little. "Now, get out of my way so I can get to work."

"Nobody expects you to fail, Desiree."

Her laugh was harsh, her eyes bright with anger and grief. "Everyone expects me to fail. I'm a woman in a profession where men rule. None of them think I have a chance in hell of running this ranch on my own. I'm going to prove them wrong."

"Is that what you think? That they're standing around like a bunch of vultures waiting for you to screw up?"

"Damn right I do. And it's not going to happen— not now and not twenty years from now." Her eyes glistened with determination as she stared into his. "There's never been a Thoroughbred ranch run by a woman before because none of the men in the business think it's possible. I'm going to prove them wrong. I'm going to make the Triple H the best ranch in the country and I'm going to do it with or without your support."

He watched, openmouthed, as she left. He finished undressing slowly, hung up his suit and Desiree's dress, slid into his own jeans and heavy sweater.

With a sigh he headed for the front door, but made a detour to the family room at the last minute. Rio was playing with his *Star Wars* figures while Willow and Dakota sat on the couch, watching cartoons with Maria.

"Everything okay in here?" he asked, planting a kiss on his daughter's cheek while he ruffled Dakota's hair.

"I want Mama," said Willow, her lower lip stuck out in an obstinate pout.

"Didn't she stop by before heading out?" he asked the housekeeper.

"No, Jesse. I wouldn't even have known she'd left if I hadn't heard the front door slam."

He reached down and scooped up his three-year-old daughter, tickling her tummy as she laughed delightedly. "Mama will be back later," he said. "She's got a lot of stuff to do today."

"Like what?"

"Like business stuff. Plus she's pretty sad right now."

"'Cuz Grandpa went to heaven?" asked five-year-old Dakota.

"Pretty much." Jesse crouched down in front of the couch, pulling eight-year-old Rio into his arms as he did. "Mama's going to be kind of busy for a while, but that doesn't mean she doesn't love you. But she's taking over for Grandpa and—"

"You mean Mom's gonna run the ranch?" asked Rio, wide-eyed.

"That's exactly what I mean. And since it's a hard job, she might not have quite as much time to play with you as she used to. But you can always come see me if you need anything or ask Maria to call down to Grandpa's—Mama's—office if you want her. Okay?"

He stared into the three solemn faces and cursed Desiree and her insane sense of duty. No one doubted that she could run the ranch fabulously—God knew Big John had been grooming her for it since birth. She could have waited a couple of days to take on her duties, spent a little time helping her family get used to the changes that were bound to come.

Not to mention the fact that she needed some time to assimilate things herself. She'd lost her father, her children had lost their beloved grandfather, and they could all benefit from her sticking close to home right now and grieving with them.

But it wasn't to be. Hours later, after the clock had struck midnight and then some, Jesse went in search of her. He and Maria had gotten the kids fed and off to bed, but all three had demanded to see their mother before they slept. He'd put them off by promising that Desiree would be there to wake them up in the morning, though the disappointment in their faces was almost more than he could bear. Particularly as he wasn't sure if Desiree would make a liar of him or not.

As he walked toward the largest stable—the one that had held Big John's office for as long as he'd been on the Triple H—Jesse inhaled the fresh scent of new grass and early spring.

Pausing at one of the outdoor corrals, he rested his hip against the fence as he surveyed the ranch that had been his home for more than fifteen years. Every corner of it held memories—quick snapshots of his time with his wife, not so pleasant remembrances of arguments with her father. If it hadn't been for Desiree, he would have left years ago to start the small, independent stable that had always been his dream. But her loyalty was to the ranch and his loyalty was, and always had been, to her.

With a sigh, he continued his trek to the stables, shaking his head at the lone light burning in the window to Big John's office. He entered the stable quietly, stopping to murmur to each of the horses in turn. He rubbed one behind the ears, fed a sugar cube to another, ran a hand down the back of a third as he crooned softly in the language of his mother and his grandfather.

"Desiree," he called softly, as he approached her father's office. "It's time to come to bed, darlin'. Everything will still be here in the morning."

When she didn't answer, a skitter of unease skated down his spine, one that had nothing to do with logic and everything to do with emotion. Some days, when he least expected it, memories of the past snuck up on him, memories of her screams for help, of finding her with her clothes ripped and her body bruised. He shook off the unpleasant memories, tried to concentrate on the present.

"Desiree," he called again, approaching the open office door. He could hear the radio playing, tuned to the classic rock station she loved. He peered in, then smiled sadly when he saw her slumped over her desk, her cheek resting on a stack of papers, her eyes closed. She was asleep, having worked herself into exhaustion. Her eyes were shadowed with dark circles, her skin so pale it was nearly translucent. A vein in her temple throbbed even as she slept, and the sight wounded him as nothing else had.

He went over to her on silent feet, reaching out a soft hand to stroke an errant lock of hair from her forehead. God, she was beautiful. Even rundown and worn-out, her beauty shone from her. It made him needy, made him ache with the desire to hold her against him, to feel her head buried against his neck and her hands tangled in his hair—habits she'd acquired early on in their relationship, habits that he'd come to depend on.

He ran a finger over the fragile skin of her cheek, a thumb over the softness of her lower lip. He savored the peace and contentment washing through him. She wasn't easy—anybody raised by Big John couldn't be—but she was fair. She was strong and determined, and most important his. And he would take care of her, whether she wanted him to or not.

Reaching an arm under her, he lifted her into his arms and began the long walk back to the house. He loved the feel of her body pressed against his, loved the idea of sheltering her body with his own.

Carrying her through the front door and up the stairs, he laid her on the bed they'd shared for nearly ten years and began stripping off her boots and jeans in an effort to make her more comfortable.

"Jesse?" Her voice was low and husky as she reached for him.

"I'm here, darlin'." He slid her jeans down her hips and moved to pull her turtleneck over her head.

"What happened?" she asked, sitting up sleepily in an effort to aid him in his task.

"Get some rest, Desiree," he murmured softly as he slipped her favorite nightshirt over her head. Made of an unattractive gray cotton, it was ancient and had been his for years before she had confiscated it. But Desiree loved it, chose to sleep in it on nights when she was feeling exhausted or overwrought or just plain ornery. "Everything will still be where you left it in the morning."

Yawning, she wrapped her arms around his neck and pulled him down with her as she sank into the softness of the feather pillows. "Stay with me?" she asked, her voice soft and uncertain.

"Always," he answered as he settled himself beside her and pulled her into his arms. He still wore his boots and all the rest of his clothes, but if she didn't mind, then neither did he.

She snuggled against him, her hand fisted in his shirt as if afraid that he would leave her at the first opportunity. "I love you." She spoke so softly he had to strain to hear her.

"Me, too, darlin'. Me, too." He pulled her more firmly against him, let his mouth skim softly over her hair as she found her spot, her head resting in the crook of his neck. "Go to sleep, Des. They'll be plenty of time to talk tomorrow morning."

"Tomorrow," she agreed, her chin pressing into his chest as she nodded.

He closed his eyes and slid into sleep with thoughts of the future drifting through his head. They had so much to talk about, so much to do—plans for the children, for the horses, for the ranch. Tomorrow, he told himself as sleep claimed him. Tomorrow would be more than soon enough.

But when he woke the next day in the early-morning darkness and reached out a hand to touch her, Desiree was gone. It was the beginning of a pattern that would become hauntingly familiar as the days and weeks and years slowly passed.

CHAPTER TEN

"WILLOW, IT'S TIME to get dressed." Desiree knocked on the closed door of her daughter's bedroom. "Anna will be here as soon as she finishes dressing, but I thought I'd come see if you needed any help."

"Thanks, Mom. Come on in."

Desiree was surprised to see all three of her children gathered. "What have you been doing in here? Don't you two have tuxes to change into?"

"We're going, Mom." Dakota headed for the door, stopping to drop a kiss on her forehead.

"What was that for?" she asked in surprise.

He shrugged, seemingly embarrassed. "How long have we got?"

"Fifteen, twenty minutes. People are already starting to arrive."

"We'll be ready." This time it was Rio who spoke, reaching out and squeezing her hand.

"You look gorgeous, Mom," Willow murmured, taking in the chic hair and makeup Felipe had done, as well as the holly-red silk dress that dipped low in back. "You certainly don't look like the average mother of the bride."

"I know." Desiree's smile was self-deprecating. "I'm still tall and gawky after all these years."

"Not gawky, Mom. Statuesque."

Desiree snorted, even as she wrapped a companionable arm around her daughter's shoulders. "You're good for my ego—do you know that?"

"We aim to please."

"That's supposed to be my line today." She paused, taking in these three incredible people who came from her and Jesse. "I'm so proud of you, Willow. So proud of all of you. You have to know that."

"I do." Willow clasped Desiree's hand in her own. "We all do."

Dakota patted Desiree's shoulder in an awkward but touching gesture. "Thanks, Mom."

"For what?"

"For being you," Rio commented huskily.

"I know I haven't done everything right—with any of you. I've been too busy, too concerned with the ranch. But I do love the three of you more than anything in this world."

"Even the Triple Crown?" Willow's expression registered her shock at her own words. "I'm sorry."

"Don't be. It's a fair question." Desiree sank onto the edge of the bed. She didn't want to have this conversation, didn't want to explain herself, to admit her flaws. But they deserved to know, and when would she have another chance? "The Triple Crown was everything to your grandfather—especially after my mother died. The idea of winning it gave his life purpose, and soon that purpose became an obsession that nearly consumed him and everyone around him."

She paused, cleared her throat. "I watched it destroy him, watched it take over everything that he once was and everything that he could be. A few weeks before he died—almost as if he knew something was going to happen to him—he called me into his office and made me promise to win it, made me swear to bring the title home."

Desiree looked each of her children in the eye. "I gave him my word. Swore to him that I would do everything in my power to win those three races."

Desiree sighed. "I knew it was a dangerous promise, knew that it could easily consume me the same way it did him. But I was young and arrogant. Invincible, at least in my own mind."

"Mom, stop." Willow pleaded desperately. "You don't have to do this."

"Oh, I don't know. I think it's long past time for me to do this. It's come to my attention recently—and quite painfully, if I'm to be truthful—that I've done to my family what I swore I'd never do. I've put you second. From the moment my father died, I've put you and your father aside until I'd accomplished what I wanted to do. Until I'd proven that I was as good as any man and brought the Triple Crown home.

"I let you grow up waiting for a mother who was only there part of the time. And here you are, all grown up, yet I'm still chasing a fool's dream. I'm still trying to prove to Big John that I'm worthy, even if I wasn't born male."

"It's okay, Mom." Rio's voice was hoarse.

"No, it's not. It's not even close to being okay." Desiree closed her eyes, tried to swallow the knot that filled her throat. "But I am sorrier than you can ever know that I let myself get so caught up in a dream that wasn't even mine that I missed so much of what you wanted to share with me."

"Don't," Dakota said. "You were always there when we needed you. Maybe you missed some of the small stuff, but the important stuff, you were always there for that."

He crouched in front of Desiree, took both of her hands in his. "Don't give up," he said fiercely. "Whatever Dad said, whatever he did, he didn't mean it. He loves you."

She shook her head. "I'm not saying this because of your father. I'm saying this because of me. I look at you three and realize that I've done you a disservice through the years. I've been so caught up in remaining loyal to my father's vision of the ranch that I forgot the loyalty that I owed the three of you."

"That's not true, Mom."

She pinned her daughter with a calm, steady stare. "Yes, it is. And I'm sorry for it. I promise, from now on, you'll see some changes around here. Changes for the positive."

"What about Dad?" Rio asked.

It took Desiree a moment to let the pain pass before she could answer. "I don't know." She shrugged, wrapped her arms around her waist as if to protect herself from a sudden chill. "But whatever happens between your father and me, I want you to know that I mean every word I've said here today. I never meant to hurt you. I can't fix the past, but I can fix the future if you'll let me."

"It's already fixed, Mom. Already forgotten." Dakota's voice was almost as hoarse as his mother's.

"You're so much more than I deserve." Desiree sniffed, straightened her shoulders. "Please know that I've always loved you and that you've always been first in my heart. What I've done, I've done to protect your legacy, our legacy. I just went about it in the wrong way."

She stared at her children for a moment, grateful for their presence. "Well, I think that's more than enough soul-searching for one afternoon." She glanced at the gold watch she wore, the one Jesse had given her for their fifteenth wedding anniversary, and gasped.

"My God, the wedding's supposed to start in less

than forty minutes." She pushed her sons toward the door. "Go get dressed and head downstairs—ASAP. I'm sure things are heating up quickly."

Without giving them a chance to say another word, she ushered them out of the room, shutting the door behind them. Turning to her daughter, she commented, "Well, let's get this show on the road."

Willow was already at her closet, unzipping the bag that held her wedding dress. "Already ahead of you. I think I can get everything on, but I'll need you to zip me up."

"And chance messing up that work of art on your head? Felipe would have my head."

Willow giggled. "No kidding."

"Can we come in?" called a voice from the doorway.

"Of course." Desiree turned to see all four of her daughter's bridesmaids at the door, resplendent in their strapless gowns of poinsettia-red silk.

"It's about time you guys got here," commented Willow. "What do I do first?"

"Jump out the window and run for the hills," came her maid of honor's sardonic reply.

"Ha-ha, very funny." Willow rolled her eyes at her best friend.

Anna shrugged. "I told you I was the wrong person for this job. I still can't fathom why you'd want to tie yourself down to the same man for the rest of your life."

"Because I get to wear this fabulous dress,"

Willow answered, completely deadpan. "Is that not reason enough?"

"You tell her, girl," cheered Sam, Willow's roommate from her freshman year in college.

"Stockings first," commented Tori. "Then we'll worry about the rest."

The next twenty minutes passed in a blur as Willow dressed to her friends' specifications. When everything was properly arranged—from the veil to the pale-blue garter—she breathed a huge sigh of relief. "I think I'm good to go."

"Not quite." Desiree reached into the bag she'd brought with her, pulled out the pearl necklace both she and her mother had worn at their own weddings. Motioning for Willow to turn around, she fastened it, dropping a quick kiss on Willow's neck when she was finished.

"And one more thing." She pulled out a small, red jeweler's box. "I saw these a couple of weeks ago and thought they'd be perfect with your dress."

Willow took the box. "What—"

"Open it."

Willow flipped the lid and gasped, as did each of the other girls in the room. "Mom, they're gorgeous. Absolutely fabulous." With trembling hands, she unfastened one of the earrings, holding the cascade of diamonds and pearls up to her ear. "What do you think?"

"I think they were made for you." Desiree blinked back the tears blooming in her eyes for what seemed like the hundredth time that day. She hated being weak and out of control, but so much had happened in the past twelve hours that her coping mechanisms didn't have a prayer of keeping up.

"Thanks, Mom." Desiree found herself crushed against her daughter.

She clung for a moment, savoring the feel of her baby in her arms. "I love you," she whispered, smoothing a hand over Willow's veiled hair.

"I love you, too, Mama." Willow pulled away, looked her straight in the eye. "I don't blame you for anything. No matter what you say, no matter what happens, I want you to know that what you gave us was more than good enough."

Choking back her own sobs now, Desiree dropped her arms and moved away. "That's enough. We're getting maudlin, and your wedding day should be happy, not bittersweet."

"Absolutely," said Tori, as she locked an arm around Willow and began herding her toward the door. "Now let's go before James thinks he's been left at the altar. You're already five minutes late."

"Have you got everything?" Sam asked, looking around the room critically.

Willow's hand closed over the journal Desiree held out for her. Willow's eyes shone with so much hope that Desiree felt her own heart lift just a little. "Where's your bouquet?" she asked huskily.

"I've got it," Anna said briskly as she opened the door, her arms full of the poinsettias Willow would carry. "Are you ready for this?"

Willow's smile was brilliant, her former doubts completely gone. "You bet."

"Then let's go find your dad," Anna said. "And remember, once you get through this, everything else is a cakewalk. In twenty-five years we'll all be sitting here celebrating your silver wedding anniversary and you'll wonder why you were ever nervous."

Willow faltered at the words, her gaze seeking her mother's. "Don't go there, baby. This day is about you and James, no one else," Desiree said.

But as she watched her daughter nod, watched her smile as she turned to walk down the wide, circular staircase, Desiree's smile faded as she remembered her own silver anniversary—less than two years before.

WILLOW GLANCED AT THE clock on the wall for the tenth time in as many minutes. "What should we do, Mom? It's close to nine and people are getting restless."

Desiree shrugged, but couldn't keep an embarrassed heat from blossoming in her cheeks. "I don't know what to do. Your father arranged to meet me here no later than seven forty-five. I've called his cell, tried the walkie-talkie but he's not answering."

"Do you want Rio and me to go look for him?" asked Dakota. "We can run over to the Cherokee and see if he's around."

Desiree stiffened at the mention of the small stable her husband had started independent of the Triple H. If he was over there instead of here, at the surprise party she'd thrown for him to celebrate their twenty-fifth wedding anniversary, she didn't know what she'd do. It was bad enough that the Triple H could no longer hold his attention; she couldn't bear to think that the same could be said about her.

"I don't think that's necessary," she demurred as she forced a smile onto her face. "We'll just forget the surprise, get the party into full swing and—"

"Without Dad?" Rio asked incredulously.

"But, Mom, we're celebrating your anniversary," Willow wailed.

"I know that!" Desiree snapped, then struggled for control. "But I don't know what else to do. When your father shows up, he can join the party. Until then, we'll just make his excuses and hope that everyone has a good time."

Looking unconvinced, her children set off to do her bidding—turning up the music, mingling with the guests while she made sure that the bar was still well stocked and that the hors d'eouvres were circulating.

The next hour and a half passed with excruciating slowness as Desiree kept her smile painted on through sheer determination. If she saw one more person staring at her with pity, she would loose her mind completely. As it was, her cheeks ached, her head throbbed and her vision kept blurring at the most inopportune times.

"Excuse me, Desiree?"

She turned at the familiar voice. "Can I get you something, Edna?" she asked, forcing a brightness into her voice and smile that she was far from feeling.

"We're going to take off," Edna replied. "I've got an early morning tomorrow. But thank you for inviting us."

"You don't have to go. Jesse will—"

Edna's smile was kind. "I'm sure he'll be here any minute and I am sorry that I'll miss him. But 4:00 a.m. comes quickly."

"Of course it does." Desiree smiled graciously, though she was screaming inside. Anger was slowly giving way to fear, and she was beginning to wonder if she should start calling the local hospitals. But wouldn't someone have called her if Jesse had been in an accident?

That first departing couple launched a mass exodus. All too soon, Desiree was left alone, staring at her children and daughter-in-law in consternation. "Well, that was a bust," she commented with a forced smile.

"I'm going to go look for him," Dakota said furiously. "He can't do this to you."

"No one's going anywhere," answered Desiree. "Your father will get home when he gets home."

"What if something's wrong?" Willow asked.

"I'll call over to Cherokee. See if he's still there," Rio volunteered.

"I'll call," Desiree insisted firmly. "Go on to bed."

"But—" Dakota interjected.

"Go." Desiree's voice was firm as she stared down her children. They wanted to argue, but adults or not, they knew better than to mess with her when she used that tone.

Desiree waited until her children had ascended the stairs before she went to the office to call Jesse. But the phone rang and rang, no matter how much she willed him to pick up. After leaving messages on both his cell and office phones, she went upstairs and changed into jeans and a long-sleeved black T-shirt. She couldn't imagine that he was at one of the ranch's stables, but she wasn't going to panic until she'd checked all the alternatives.

As she let herself into the house twenty-five minutes later, she acknowledged that maybe it really was time to let go of the anger and begin to seriously worry. She glanced at the clock on the living room mantel—12:15 a.m.—and no word from Jesse. It wasn't like him to be so careless on a normal day, so she had trouble imagining him being deliberately callous on their twenty-fifth wedding anniversary.

Uneasy, she walked back to the office, her teeth worrying her lower lip as she went. Indecision clawed at her—should she start calling the hospitals or wait a little longer? Should she call some of Jesse's friends to find out if, for some reason, they had seen him? But most of his friends had been guests at tonight's calamitous party, so she had trouble believing he was with any of them.

Rubbing her hands over her eyes as she sank into her desk chair, she stared at the phone willing it to ring. But it remained silent, and the uneasiness coalesced into a sick feeling in the pit of her stomach. With a groan of dismay she turned and grabbed the phone book off the bottom of her bookshelf.

Which hospital would he go to? Which one would they rush him to if he'd had an accident? Panic welled, but she ruthlessly beat it back as she reached for the phone. There was no reason to lose it until she found out what had actually happened to him.

She was dialing the numbers to the third hospital—having struck out with the first two—when she heard the front door open. Frantic, she ran for the hall. "Where have you been?" she demanded, skidding to a halt inches from her husband. Her eyes ran over him from head to toes, checking for injuries. "Are you all right? I've been so worried."

"Why?" he asked, casually slipping out of his jacket and reaching for a hanger from the closet.

Her mouth fell open. "Because you're almost five hours late. Because it's our anniversary. Because the kids and I threw a surprise party for you that you didn't bother to show up for."

"Why would you throw a party?" he asked calmly, stepping past her and heading for the stairs.

"Where are you going?"

"To bed. I'm tired."

She trailed him up the stairs, nearly speechless with anger. "Without any kind of an explanation? I don't think so."

"I'm tired, Des. And I've got an early morning tomorrow."

"What is wrong with you?" She reached for him but he turned away before she touched him. A sliver of hurt cut through the anger and bewilderment.

"I've had a long day and I'd like to go to sleep." He shrugged out of his shirt, headed for the bathroom to clean up.

"Well, I've had an even longer day, and no one's sleeping until I get some answers." She got in front of him, held her ground though he tried to sweep past her. "I was calling the hospitals, Jesse."

She saw a flicker of guilt cross his face—but it was there and gone so fast she wasn't sure she hadn't imagined it. "I was worried. I couldn't imagine that you would voluntarily come home after midnight on our twenty-fifth wedding anniversary."

"Desiree—"

"Talk to me, Jess. Tell me what was so damned important that you couldn't make it home until after our anniversary was over."

She looked at him beseechingly, myriad emotions battling for a stronghold inside of her. But until he responded, until she knew why he had avoided coming home, she wouldn't know which emotion she should let gain control or even if she would have that choice.

He started to speak, his black eyes glittering with things she refused to name. But then he shook his head, turned away, splashed water on his face and through his hair.

She stood to the side and watched him. It was painfully obvious that he wanted her to leave. She started to do just that, but suddenly she couldn't tear her eyes away from him.

The well-developed muscles of his back rippled with his every movement, as did the ones on his stomach. Desire curled through her, adding one more bewildering emotion to her already heightened senses.

How many men actually had a six-pack at Jesse's age? It wasn't natural, wasn't sane—it certainly wasn't fair that he could make her want him this much without even trying. She wanted to rage at him until he'd given her an explanation for his bizarre behavior. But part of her was so happy, so grateful, that he was whole and well that she couldn't help the sudden awareness of him that sprang to life inside of her.

Desiree stepped closer, trailed a finger down his spine. She felt him stiffen against her seconds before he turned and caught her wrist in his strong fingers.

"What are you doing?" His voice was lower, huskier than it had been mere minutes before.

"I thought that was obvious." Her voice was breathier, more teasing than it had been. She twisted her wrist in his hand, a small feminine gesture that accomplished her immediate release.

She reached for the hem of her shirt, raised it to expose her flat stomach. She saw his eyes darken even more, an answering response roaring to life in him before he could stop it.

"I thought you were angry."

"You're alive and unharmed when I was imagining the worst. I'm grateful." She spoke no less than the truth, though anger and hurt were still running a close second to the desire thrumming through her. She wanted to touch him, taste him, reassure herself on a purely primitive level that he was all right.

"Jake called me." He admitted it grudgingly. "One of his horses was sick and the doctor couldn't figure out what was wrong with him. He wanted me to…" He stopped as she tugged her top over her head, revealing the hot-pink demi-bra she'd bought last weekend in the hopes of generating just such a response.

He trailed hot fingers over her full breasts where they spilled over the top of the cups. "You're so beautiful."

"So are you." She arched against him, giving him better access, and he took it with a groan. His lips skimmed down her neck, over her collarbone, pausing at the hollow of her throat. She moaned as his tongue darted out, licking slowly, softly, turning her knees to mush beneath her. "Jesse—"

"Desiree," he murmured, his eyes dark and wicked even as he allowed his hands to cup her breasts, his thumbs to stroke the nipples barely covered by the lace of the demi-bra. He lowered his head and feasted, his tongue flicking over the hard nubs of her nipples again and again until she cried out, her knees actually giving way beneath her.

He caught her, swept her up in his arms and carried her to the bed. "I'm sorry." He breathed the words against her hair as he lowered himself on top of her. "I was stupid, an ass."

He felt so good above her—so hard and hot—that she couldn't stop herself from moving against him, her legs widening as she sought a deeper connection. "It's okay," she heard herself gasp as she pulled his head down to hers. "The horse—

"Didn't need me as much as you did. I should have been here." His lips brushed hers, once, twice, before skimming down to her breasts. His tongue followed the line where the top of her breasts met the bra in a teasing, tasting, tickling exploration.

She laughed huskily, her fingers going to the waistband of his jeans, dipping inside to stroke him, reveling at how quickly he had become hard. He groaned and thrust against her questing fingers, even as his hands reached down to still them. "I need a shower," he murmured. "I've been in the stables all day."

"I like the way you smell," she answered truthfully, slowly unzipping his pants.

He sprang free and she reached for him, running her lips and tongue along him in leisurely strokes. She loved how he quivered with each touch of her mouth, loved the power she had over this strong, tough man. She took her time, played with him, stroked him with her hands and lips and tongue until she felt his muscles tremble.

His hands tangled in her hair and he groaned before he could stop himself. "Desi…" His voice was low and pleading, his hands urgent, and she knew she had pushed him to the limit. With a murmur of pure pleasure, she took him in her mouth and let her tongue swirl over and around him.

All too soon Jesse was pulling away, ignoring her protests.

"Jesse—"

"Shh," he murmured, slowly pulling off her jeans and hot pink panties. "I need to be inside you.

"But—"

"Relax," he said as he flipped her onto her stomach. And then his fingers were everywhere, kneading the kinks from her lower back, from the top of her thighs, skimming closer and closer to the heart of her.

She squirmed restlessly, arching into him. "Jesse, please!" she wailed, too far gone to be patient.

"Now?" he asked, pulling her to her knees and stroking a finger along her silken folds.

"Yes, now," she whimpered, pressing her back to his front. "Please, now!"

He positioned her, and with a groan sank home. She pushed against him, meeting each of his thrusts, more wild and needy than she could ever remember being. Tension built in her, coiling higher and higher until she was sobbing Jesse's name. He circled her hips with his right arm, pulling her more fully against him as his thumb found and stroked the knot of her desire.

She exploded, her body convulsing as wave after wave of pleasure slammed through her. She felt him stiffen against her, felt the pulses of his release move through her, intensifying her pleasure, making it last and last until she collapsed, all but comatose, onto the bed.

Consciousness returned slowly and Desiree became aware of Jesse's heart beating heavily beside her as his hands tangled in her hair. She turned her head and found herself staring into his worried, midnight-dark eyes. She wanted to soothe him, to stroke a hand down his cheek and tell him that it was okay. That she understood. But she couldn't, because it wasn't and she didn't.

She cleared her throat, found her voice. "Why didn't you call?" she asked before she even knew she was going to ask. "I would have understood."

"I didn't know what to say."

"What do you mean?" A chill swept through her and she reached for the comforter, her nudity bothering her for the first time that she could remember. "The horse—"

"Was an excuse." He sighed heavily, ran a hand through his untamed hair. "I knew what was wrong before I got there."

She studied him with puzzled eyes. "Then why…" Her voice trailed off. She was suddenly too afraid of the answer to ask the question.

"I didn't want to face you." He stood abruptly, went to his dresser where he pulled on a pair of sweats with his back to her.

"I love you, Desiree." The words seemed ripped from him.

"Why do you say that like it's a bad thing?" she asked, crossing the room to wrap her arms around him from behind. "I love you, too."

He turned, his eyes dark and worried as he studied

her. Then he was moving away, reaching for a T-shirt and tugging it on as he headed for the door.

She stared at him, bewildered. "Where are you going?"

He shook his head, opened the door. "I can't do this now."

"Do what?"

"Go to bed, Desi. I'll be up later." He closed the door as he slipped from the room.

She stared after him for a long time, then walked to the bathroom and cleaned herself up before slipping into a nightgown and crawling into bed. Her mind spun with questions but she refused to chase after him. So she lay in bed, staring at the ceiling, unable to sleep but too emotionally exhausted to do anything else.

When Jesse finally came to bed, hours later, she was still awake. She wanted to reach for him but couldn't find a way to span the sudden distance between them. She waited for him to turn to her, to wrap her in his arms and pull her against him as he had every night for twenty-five years.

When morning came she was still waiting.

CHAPTER ELEVEN

TEARS LEAKED FROM THE corner of his eye despite himself as he surveyed his daughter in her wedding dress. The fact that Desiree remained dry-eyed next to him only made his lack of control more annoying. The music started—a Spanish guitar version of some love song that sounded familiar but he couldn't place—and he watched the bridal party get into position.

"Are you ready?" his daughter asked, clutching his arm with one cold hand.

"As ready as I'm going to get," he answered, watching first his wife, then Willow's bridesmaids, precede them up the aisle.

When Anna finally got to the front, the melodic strains of the guitar switched to the bridal march. He felt Willow tense next to him.

"We can still duck out the back," he whispered to her, even as he straightened and prepared to take that first step forward.

"Too late," she giggled as she took a deep breath. "I love you, Daddy."

Jesse's heart clenched, skipping a beat or two before he could steady himself. "I love you, too, baby." He tried to be surreptitious as he wiped at his eye, but he looked up just in time to see Willow smiling indulgently at him.

"All right, all right," he muttered. "Let's do this thing before I change my mind about giving my only daughter away."

The walk up the aisle was a fusion of faces and memories. He couldn't help remembering the day his daughter was born. The first time he held her. The first time he put her on a horse. The first time she'd ever had her heart broken. She'd been his for so long—his baby, his little girl—that giving her away now was a lot harder than he'd ever anticipated.

Then they were at the front and all he could do was kiss her cheek as he handed her off to another man. He made a wish for her happiness then took his seat next to Desiree, trying his best to look as if it wasn't the last place he wanted to be.

Desiree reached out a hand, laid it on his knee. "She looks beautiful, doesn't she?"

Waves of heat spread through him, radiating from his knee, warming him in a way that made a mockery of his anger. He stared, transfixed for a moment, at the delicate hand that was as familiar to him as his own. She'd done something to her nails—they were

long and half-white and seemed out of place on her
strong but delicate fingers.

He clasped for her hand, savoring the feel of her
soft skin as it rubbed against his tough and callused
palm. She had such small hands—palm to palm, her
fingers barely reached the knuckles of his own—it
amazed him still that she could hold a bucking horse
or a crooked businessman in the palm of them. She'd
always done a hell of a job of holding him in them,
as well—wrapping him around her little finger,
keeping him under her thumb.

The familiar fury burned through him and he stiffened, dropping her hand as if it had suddenly burned
him. How could she do this to him with just a word,
just a touch? How could she make him wish things
were different, even after he'd found out how deeply
her betrayal ran?

"Jesse?" Her voice was low, her cheeks red as she
stared at him with dismayed eyes.

"Yes, Desiree. Willow looks very beautiful." The
words were stilted, almost painful, but he couldn't do
any better. Not with everything that lay between
them. Not with that damn newspaper article burning
through his brain like a wildfire.

He turned away before she could say more,
angling his shoulders so that his back was almost
completely toward her. She gasped, but he resisted
the temptation to look, just as he resisted the in-

stinctive need to apologize. She was the one who had hurt him, he reminded himself. She was the one who had spent the last five, ten, even fifteen years of their life together giving everything she had to the ranch so that there was nothing left over for him, for them.

The ceremony passed in a blur. He stood at the right places, sat when everyone else did. He heard his daughter take her vows, watched her new husband lean down to kiss her, but nothing seemed real. He watched it all from a distance, as if a glass wall separated him from everyone else in the garden.

Then it was over and they were heading to the ballroom for the reception. People were stopping him, congratulating him, chatting him up, and for the first time in his life he was grateful for the need to socialize. It made the distance between Desiree and himself less noticeable.

The hours passed quickly. Food and liquor flowed freely, laughter and joy even more so. He had no appetite, but ate and drank because it was expected of him. Because Desiree's eyes were on him and his stupid pride wouldn't allow her to see how much he was hurting. The divorce had been his idea, after all.

He danced the first dance with his wife, the second with his daughter. As he held Willow in his arms and looked down at her glowing face, some of the ice that had formed around him melted.

"You look happy, baby," he murmured as he pulled her close.

"I am, Daddy, happier than I ever thought possible."

"Then I guess I've got to get used to the fact that you're not my little girl anymore." He kissed her cheek. "Things are changing so fast."

A small frown appeared on Willow's face. "She really loves you, you know."

He stiffened. "I'm not discussing this with you, Willow."

Her eyes narrowed, and for a moment she looked so much like her mother that it took his breath away. "Well, I'm discussing it with you. You hurt her, Daddy. I know you didn't mean to, but you did." She looked over at Desiree, who wore a broad smile that didn't reach her eyes. "Can't you see how devastated she is?"

"My relationship with your mother is none of your business."

"It is when I see how sad you both are. Whatever you've done, it can still be fixed."

"Whatever *I've* done?"

She sighed heavily. "Yes, Dad. Whatever you've done. I know she isn't the easiest person to live with, that she's obsessed with the ranch and the horses and the stupid Triple Crown. But…" She paused.

"Don't stop now."

She eyed him with unconcealed frustration. It was the same look she'd been giving him since she was two and he'd refused to let her ride one of the champion Thoroughbreds. He couldn't help smiling at her impatience.

"I wasn't planning to. You've got to remember she was raised by Big John. A lot of who she is and what she wants comes from him, whether she wants it to or not."

"Willow—"

"All right, all right. I won't say anything else." But her eyes gleamed when she reached into a hidden pocket on the side of her dress. "But in exchange, I need you do me a favor?"

He eyed her warily. His youngest was not above subterfuge if it would get her her way. "What do you want me to do?"

Her smile was brilliant as she handed him a blue book. "Give this to Mom for me. I'm afraid I'll forget and it'll get lost."

His eyebrows pulled together as he examined the book more closely. "What is it?"

"She'll know. Just tell her thank-you and that I didn't want to lose it."

The music stopped. "I'm going to go find my husband." She giggled. "My husband," she repeated. "I really love the way that sounds."

His smile was indulgent while he watched her walk away, but the indulgence quickly faded to puzzlement as he studied the book in his hands. There was no title on the front, nothing on the spine. What kind of book was it and what could be so important about it that Willow was carrying it around on her wedding day?

He cracked the cover and started in surprise when he saw the sloping perfection of Desiree's handwriting. Eyes narrowed, he skimmed the first page, barely noticing the hollow feeling suddenly invading his stomach. Someone bumped into him and he shoved the book guiltily into his pocket before moving as far from the dance floor as possible.

He wanted to escape from the crowded room, leaving the festivities far behind as he settled down to read the words his wife had written so many years before. He wouldn't, of course. Willow would kill him if he ducked out of her wedding festivities before she and her husband did. But the journal was burning a hole in his pocket despite his best intentions, commanding his attention when he should be focusing on socializing and making sure that everything was going smoothly.

He went through the motions for the rest of the evening, laughing with old friends and acquaintances. Talking a little business when he couldn't avoid it. Dancing with his daughter and hanging with his sons when he could.

But eventually Willow and James left on their honeymoon amid showers of bubbles and good wishes. The guests slowly began to leave until only the cleaning and catering staff and his family remained.

"My God, my feet hurt," Desiree muttered, slipping out of the four inch heels she'd been wearing for the last six hours.

"Mine, too," commented Brooke, as she followed suit.

"Then why wear shoes like that?" asked Rio. "There must have been ones with lower heels you could have gotten."

"But they wouldn't have looked nearly as good," answered his mother with a mock frown. "And you know us Rainwater women—we're all about vanity."

All five of them burst into laughter. "You've been a lot of things in your life, Mom," commented Dakota. "Vain has never been one of them."

"Isn't that the truth?" Desiree inclined her head ruefully. "Of course, that's probably because I've never had anything to be vain about."

"That's not true." The words burst from Jesse before he could stop them. "You're beautiful. You've always been beautiful."

Desiree's eyes widened as they met his. Electricity arced between them, powerful and intense, and her laugh, when it came, was awkward. "Yeah, right. I'm a regular cover model—all six gangly feet of me."

Rio cleared his throat, disturbed more than he wanted to admit by the sudden tension streaming between his parents. "Do you need any help cleaning up, Mom?" he asked.

Jesse watched as she broke their contact and focused on their son. "Go on to bed, all of you." She included Jesse in her sweeping motion. "I'm just going to stay and make sure the caterers get things packed up and get off all right. The rest can be cleaned up tomorrow."

"We can stay and help," Brooke offered, though she swayed with exhaustion. "With all of us working—"

"Rio, take your wife up to bed. She looks like she's going to drop," Jesse interrupted. "You go, too, Dakota. Your mom and I can handle this."

When the kids had left, Desiree turned to him. "You don't need to stay. I can handle things, really."

He studied her, noticing her pallor and the dark circles under her eyes for the first time. "You look exhausted." His tone was more accusatory than he liked.

She stared at him in disbelief as her hands clenched into fists by her sides. "It's been a long day, Jesse. Filled with surprises," she said shakily.

Guilt hit him hard, a quick punch to the gut that nearly had him doubling over. He had done this to her. He had ruined their daughter's wedding day with his impulsiveness.

He wanted to say something to erase the haunted look in her eyes. It had been his intention to have it out with her tonight; he had planned on confronting her and demanding an explanation about Tom Bradford. But she looked so tired, so beaten, that he couldn't bring himself to kick her when she was down. Tomorrow was soon enough to deal with things between them. He knew her well enough to know that by tomorrow all of her defenses would be back in place.

"Go to bed, Desi." His voice was husky with everything that had been left unsaid. "I'll pay the caterers."

"I can take care of it—"

"Damn it, Desiree. I know you can take care of it. I know you can do everything. But you're dead on your feet. Go to bed and let me take care of this for you."

She froze at his tone, her eyes growing wider. When she spoke, her voice was stilted. "Okay, then. Thank you." Her bare feet whispered across the floor as she all but ran for the door.

He stared after her, cursing himself. He'd hurt her again, though he hadn't meant to. When had she gotten so sensitive? He laughed unpleasantly. When had he become such a bastard?

He grabbed a beer from behind the bar before sinking into a chair in the corner, as far out of the way as he could get from where the catering staff was packing up. He popped the top and took a long swallow before propping his feet on a nearby seat.

Silently contemplating the beer, he brooded as he listened to the activity going on around him. Long

minutes passed before he remembered the book
Willow had given him. Desiree's journal. He pulled it
out of his pocket to stare at it. He wanted to open it and
read what was inside. But he wasn't sure, even after all
these years, that he could handle it. That he could deal
with Desiree's true opinion of the ranch and of him.

Eventually he did open it, of course, because he
could do nothing else. He read the first entry quickly,
his eyes widening with disbelief as he skimmed her
thoughts on love, on destiny. Page after page, he was
shocked and abruptly humbled by this rare glimpse
into his wife's mind. Perhaps that's what his daughter
had had in mind when she'd handed it to him.

He read voraciously, stopping only when his gaze
fell on a date he couldn't bear to remember. He nearly
closed the book, nearly walked away from it to avoid
reading his wife's thoughts about what had happened
on August 6, 2006. It was a day he had come to think
of as the beginning of the end of their marriage. He'd
lived and relived it in his thoughts and dreams nearly
every night for the past two years, and he really didn't
want to read about it from Desiree's point of view.

But he'd never been a coward, had never walked
away from the more unpleasant tasks in life. So, with
a grimace and a long swallow of beer, he began to read.

How do you take back what you say in anger?
How do you fight a battle that seems completely

unwinnable? I'm so tired that I don't know if I can fight anymore. How can anyone be this tired at forty-seven—tired and angry and so disgusted with myself that I can barely look at myself in the mirror or my husband in the eye?

Things had been going so well. Rio had just come home from school and was working on the ranch. Jesse and I had managed to smooth out so many of the rough edges that have crept into our marriage through the years. Then I went and ruined it. No, we ruined it, because he must take at least partial responsibility for what has happened.

We lost the Triple Crown again—a state of affairs that I am becoming embarrassingly familiar with. Our quest for the title and the near misses, year after year, have even sparked a kind of folklore around the track. Tales of a jinx, a curse, a self-fulfilling prophecy that will keep us from ever winning those three races in one year.

I don't believe in superstition and I don't believe in curses, but as I wait, year after year, to fulfill my father's dying wish, I admit it gets tougher and tougher to still believe.

I did something horrible, said things I am completely ashamed of now that the heat of anger has passed me by. But how do I take them back? How do I approach him and say that I am sorry? Where will we be if I can't?

When did marriage get so difficult? When did a collective dream cease to be enough and individual dreams spring up to take its place? I want a Triple Crown. I want to fulfill my promise to my father. Jesse doesn't understand, because he wasn't raised by Big John. He doesn't understand this burning need inside of me not to screw up, not to live down to my father's expectations of me.

How could following my own needs and desires, how could becoming the best woman I knew how to be, be such a complete disappointment to him? I married Jesse because I loved him and I couldn't imagine my life without him—a feeling that still holds true today, even after every bitter word that's passed between us and every disappointment we've been for each other. It is only after I've fought with my husband month after month, year after year, that the real question has become clear to me. How have I let the needs and ideas of a prejudiced old man rule the life I've spent so many years trying to build? How have I let my father interfere so completely in my relationship with my husband, with my children, with everyone I know?

We lost the Triple Crown today and I am so ashamed of what I said, of how I acted. I accused Jesse of sabotage, of betrayal, though I didn't believe the words coming out of my mouth even as I said them. But he did. I could see it in his eyes, see it in the pain and disgust and—hatred?—that stared back at me. I told him he had betrayed me, betrayed the ranch, betrayed our entire family, when the truth is I'm the one who's betrayed him—over and over again. I'm the one who's let everything come between us, the one who's pushed him away when all he wanted was to take care of me, to be close to me.

We lost the Triple Crown today when my horse came in second at the Belmont Stakes, second to Jesse's horse, Delilah, from his new stable, his new brainchild, his new love, Cherokee Dreaming. I've never felt so incompetent, so angry, so downright foolish—what is he not getting from the Triple H, what am I not giving him, that he feels the need to start his own line?

We lost the Triple Crown today and as I stared my husband down, terrible accusations trembling on my lips, I couldn't help but wonder if we'd lost something infinitely more precious.

JESSE DIDN'T WANT TO face Desiree, didn't know what to begin to say to her. Things weren't supposed to work out this way. Delilah was a great racehorse with a huge heart and the love of running, but she was a late bloomer, a late starter. It had been a miracle that she'd qualified for Belmont at all, a miracle that all of his plans had come together so smoothly.

Months ago he'd noticed that Born Lucky ran best when Delilah was beside her. They brought out the best in each other, pushed each other, challenged each other, saw in each other something that made them both run faster and better than they had ever run alone. He'd worked hard—incredibly hard—to get Delilah into this race to help pull Lucky out of the funk she'd descended into. As he'd clocked them on the training circles these past few weeks, he'd even come to dream of a one-two finish. But in his dreams Born Lucky was always first, with Delilah a close second. The reality had been the reverse and the consequences worse than he even wanted to contemplate.

He'd taken his turn in the winner's circle as owner instead of trainer—a little thrill ran through him at the thought, though he quickly tamped it down—had taken care of the horses, had talked to the press as well as friends, acquaintances and even his kids as he'd searched the throngs of people for his wife. But Desiree was nowhere to be found, which is why he'd finally returned to the hotel, angry and upset...and just nervous enough to be disgusted with himself.

The suite was empty, though Desiree's clothes still hung in the closet and her toiletries still sat on the bathroom vanity. He tried to ignore the relief that swept through him, to pretend that he hadn't been afraid she'd taken her things and cut out of town as fast as possible.

He grabbed a cola from the minibar and, after kicking off his boots, sank gratefully onto the plush sofa. He let his head fall back, closed his eyes and tried to block everything out for at least a few minutes.

Less than five minutes later the door to the hotel suite crashed open and he jumped despite himself. He turned to see Desiree breathing fire, so angry that she was noticeably shaking. "How could you?" The accusation whipped through the room.

He put out a placating hand. "Let me explain."

"Explain?" she asked in a voice that cut like razors. "What's there to explain, Jesse? You deliberately sabotaged the Triple H, deliberately put in one of your precious horses to keep us from winning."

Though he'd been expecting the accusations, had prepared for them even, they still hurt and angered him. "Do you really believe that?"

"What else am I supposed to believe?"

"You could trust me."

Her laugh was harsh, and incredibly painful to

hear. "You stabbed me in the back in front of hundreds of thousands of people and now you're telling me I should trust you?"

"It wasn't like that, Desiree. Things didn't work out like I had planned."

"Oh, I think they worked out exactly as you planned. What I want to know is why? What did I do that was so bad you felt the need to humiliate me this way?"

"Humiliate you?"

"Yes, you humiliated me. Do you have any idea how many people have given me pitying looks this afternoon? Do you have any idea how many snide comments I've had to deal with about controlling my husband, or worse, controlling the hired help?"

"Excuse me?" His voice dripped ice. "Since when has our marriage been about controlling each other?"

"Don't you twist my words." Her eyes narrowed.

"I don't think I had to twist them—you did a fine job of that yourself."

"I refuse to be the one put on the defensive here. You're the one who entered a ringer into the race. You stole the Triple Crown right out from under me."

He stared at her incredulously. "When did this get to be all about you, Desiree? When did the rest of us fall by the wayside?"

"The day my husband betrayed me." She glared at him with enough hatred to stop his heart. "You know how much this meant to me. That race was ours—no one else would have been able to touch Lucky and you know it."

"What exactly are you accusing me of?"

She pulled herself up to her full height and somehow managed to look down her nose at him, though he stood a good four inches taller than she. "I think it's obvious, isn't it? All these years I've put my faith in you. I've ignored the gossip that said you didn't have it in you to deliver this title. All these years, I've trusted you. But now I can't help but wonder if that trust was misplaced. Have we lost all these years because of bad luck? Or have you been sabotaging us all along?"

There was a roaring in his ears. His chest was so tight he would have worried he was having a heart attack if he could think of anything but Desiree and her insane accusations. "You don't mean that."

"Oh, yes, I do."

"Stop it, Desiree, before you say something you can't take back."

"I haven't said anything I would want to take back."

Fury filled him, burning hotter and more vicious than it ever had before. He opened his mouth, prepared to deliver a scathing retort and lay into her like she so richly deserved. But he choked back the words at the last minute, refusing to lower himself to her level.

He walked into the bedroom and closed the door behind him. His fists were clenched, his breathing harsh, as he struggled to get himself under control. He just needed some time—a minute, a few seconds, anything to give himself a chance to calm down. To get the image of strangling her out of his head.

The bedroom door slammed open. "Don't you walk away from me."

"Get out."

"Don't you dare tell me to get out. I am paying for this suite, just like I pay for everything. Your salary, the house you live in, the food you eat."

The roaring grew louder. Desiree, eyes wide, had clamped her hand over her mouth as soon as the words had escaped. He could see the apology in her eyes, but it was too late. The damage was done.

"Jesse, I didn't mean—"

"Oh, don't back down now, darlin'. You'll lose all your momentum."

"I'm sorry. It just came out. I…" She looked ill as she made the excuses, but he was far past caring.

"I'll move Cherokee Dreaming off the ranch as soon as we get back."

"You don't have to do that."

"Oh, yes, I do. As for the rest…" He shrugged. "I guess it's up to you. I spent the first years of our marriage trying to convince you to move off the Triple H. I wanted to build a home for us and our children using my own money. I didn't have as much as your father, especially back then, but it would have been enough. I would have built you the nicest house I could."

"I know." Her voice was anguished.

"You don't know anything. If you did, you never would have had the nerve to throw that in my face."

He crossed to the dresser, scooped a pair of jeans, clean underwear and a red polo shirt from the top drawer.

"Where are you going?" she asked.

"To get my own room. One you aren't paying for."

"Jesse, no." Her voice was low and urgent. "You can't."

"It's a little too late for you to tell me what I can or can't do," he replied as he headed toward the door. "Besides, you don't expect any of your other employees to sleep with the boss."

CHAPTER TWELVE

WITH A SIGH OF DISGUST, Desiree gave up watching the minutes crawl by on the digital clock next to her bed. Emotionally and physically exhausted from the wedding, she had lain in bed for nearly two hours waiting in vain for sleep to claim her. Throwing the covers back, she climbed out of bed and pulled on a pair of sweats and a T-shirt. If she couldn't sleep, she might as well do something useful. She had forgotten to check on M.C. before heading to bed, so she would do so now.

The house was quiet as she let herself out the front door—she had heard the caterers leave over an hour earlier and had listened as Jesse climbed the stairs and headed to his room down the hall. She'd wanted to go to him, had wanted to crawl into bed next to him and ask him to hold her, but her pride wouldn't allow it.

As she neared the maternity stable, she heard the high-pitched screams of a horse in pain. M.C. was in labor and no one had alerted her. She started to run, hitting the stable at full speed.

"I thought I told you to call me," she said as soon as she entered the stable, expecting to find her stable manager with the frightened mare.

But it was Jesse's voice that answered her, Jesse her eyes found as she searched the dim stable. "I figured you could use the sleep. I can handle this."

"I know you can," she answered softly as she approached the laboring horse. "But I wanted to be here."

His eyes met hers in the semidarkness, concern gleaming in their ebony depths. "Then have a seat. It's going to be a long few hours."

Desiree settled into the straw next to M.C. and reached a hand out to stroke her shuddering stomach. Her breaths were coming in pants, and contractions strained her body almost continuously. "Is she all right?"

"She's in a lot of pain and the foal isn't in any hurry to drop. But I've checked and it's positioned correctly—not breech or anything."

Desiree sighed in relief. "Thank God. I know you can handle just about anything, but I'm glad we don't have to deal with that tonight on top of everything else."

Jesse's startled eyes met hers, and she wondered what she'd said that could have surprised him. Then she realized—she had shocked him with her faith in him. Had she praised him so rarely in recent years? Did he really not know how much respect she had for him and his abilities?

"What can I do?" Her voice was subdued when she spoke.

"Just talk to her, pet her. I need to check her again and she hates it."

Desiree leaned down, pressed her cheek to the top of M.C.'s head as she crooned to her in the language and the words she'd heard Jesse use so often. She could tell the minute Jesse had started to examine the horse because she tensed, her shaking getting much worse.

Desiree grimaced before she could stop herself. Labor was hard on any horse, but it was especially bad for the high-strung and coddled Thoroughbreds, who were so unused to painful disruptions in their daily lives. "What a good girl you are, M.C.," she crooned. "Your baby's going to be so beautiful. All long legs and curiosity. He'll be a champion, just like you, girl. Just like you."

She was conscious of Jesse's eyes on her and the frown that seemed to have taken up permanent residence on his face. There had been so many days—years really—when he'd never looked at her with anything but a smile that this new countenance was hard to take.

She didn't know how long they sat there, with Jesse murmuring to M.C. in Cherokee while Desiree continued to pet and sooth her. But suddenly Jesse's crooning stopped and he said grimly, "Okay, this is it."

Desiree moved to her knees, taking M.C.'s head

in her hand as she did. "All right, girl. Let's show him how it's done."

The mare's whinny was high-pitched and painful to hear. Her body shuddered again and again as she struggled to bring forth new life. Jesse continued to work, using his strong arms to help M.C. guide her foal into the world.

As the horse continued to shake, her body convulsing, Desiree closed her eyes and prayed. "Should it be taking this long?" she asked Jesse hoarsely.

"Some take longer than others," he said. "But she's looking good. God willing, they'll both be fine."

Suddenly M.C. gave a great push—Desiree could feel her body straining right along with the horse's— and Jesse shouted jubilantly. "Here he comes!"

Within minutes it was done, and Desiree watched the new colt struggle to his feet with tears in her eyes. He wobbled to his mother on unsteady legs, and M.C. nuzzled him, wrapping her body around him as she began to clean him.

"He's beautiful," she whispered, watching the new mother and her baby.

"Isn't he, though?" Jesse was at the big sink, washing up. "But I wouldn't expect anything less with his pedigree."

"No kidding. Talk about a champion in training."

Jesse turned to her as he dried his arms and hands. "Are you ready to head up to the house? Give Mama and her baby a little privacy?" His voice was stilted, and she could tell that it had taken a lot for him to extend such an olive branch.

"Absolutely," she answered, laying a soft hand on his back. "Just let me run by my office and get a folder I want to work on in the morning."

"All right."

She was conscious of Jesse's eyes on her as she jogged to her office. She was moving as quickly as she could without flat-out running, afraid that if she didn't hustle Jesse would get tired of waiting and head home without her. And she didn't want this fragile peace between them to end, couldn't bear for him to go back to looking at her with contempt.

Grabbing the file, Desiree started to head to the maternity barn but stopped when she saw Jesse leaning against a tree, a few feet away from where she stood. Tears sprang to her eyes and she impatiently wiped them away. She'd cried more in the past day than she had in the past thirty years, and she was beginning to feel as though she'd sprung a leak.

"Did I take too long?" she asked as she approached him.

"No." He shrugged. "I was done and figured it was just as easy to meet you here."

She nodded, smiling shyly at her husband of twenty-seven years. "Thanks for waiting."

They began to walk slowly up to the house, not

deliberately touching but so close that their shoulders occasionally brushed. Heat shot through her with every touch and she wanted to reach for his hand, wanted to hold him to her and beg him to reconsider. She'd made so many plans for the future for the ranch and for their marriage.

"Jesse—" Her voice broke despite her best intentions. She wanted to start again but suddenly lost her nerve.

He looked at her inquisitively, but she couldn't speak around the sudden lump in her throat. While the silence continued, stretched between them with the weight of things unsaid, he reached into his jacket pocket and handed her a book. "Willow asked me to return this to you. She was afraid it would get lost in the confusion."

Desiree's gaze met his in the dim light. Had he read her journal? A combination of dread and excitement curled in her stomach. If he had read it, then she'd have nothing left—no pride, no privacy, nothing at all to hide behind.

But at least he would know how much she loved him. Her eyes searched his, wanting to know. Needing to know. But he was giving nothing away.

"Thank you," she murmured, tightly clasping the book in her suddenly nerveless hands.

"No problem." He opened the front door, gestured for her to precede him. They lingered in the foyer for a few long moments. Desiree knew her feelings were in her eyes, prayed that Jesse cared enough to read them there. He didn't say anything, simply turned away and headed for the stairs.

"I'm beat. Can we talk in the morning?" he asked.

"Talk?" she asked hesitantly.

"About the conditions of the divorce?"

Desiree's already fragmented heart shattered. She actually felt it break. But if pride was all she had left, she'd be damned if she'd let him see how much he could still hurt her. "Of course. I'm just going to drop this off and then I'm heading up, as well."

"Good night." Jesse's voice sounded hoarse, but she was too distraught to care.

"Yeah." Her lips curved wryly. "Good night."

The pain was sharp, unbearable. After all these years, was this really how things were going to end? With a silence that couldn't be broken?

No. Hell, no. If this was the last chance she had to fight for her marriage, then she would fight for it. To hell with her pride. Dropping the files on the table in the middle of the foyer, she headed up the stairs after her husband.

The sound of water running through the old pipes gave testimony to the fact that he was still as awake as she was.

With a sigh, she turned left, knowing that she could be letting herself in for even more heartbreak.

But the fighter in her refused to let her marriage slip quietly away. She knocked on his door softly, not wanting to wake up the rest of the house. She grimaced. More like she didn't want to be humiliated in front of her children and Maria.

When he didn't answer and the water continued to run, she slowly turned the doorknob, relieved to find it unlocked. She called his name as she entered the room, but there was no answer. Despite her best intentions, her eyes went to the steam-filled bathroom.

She knew she should leave. She could talk to him in the morning after they'd both had a chance to get some sleep. But the huge distance between them had been bridged in the walk home from the stable tonight—at least for a little while—and she was reluctant to let it go.

She was one step away from settling herself on the bed to wait for him when her wicked streak raised its curious head. What would Jesse do if she slipped into the shower with him? Would he toss her out or welcome her as he had so many times? There was only one way to find out and, while her pride smarted at the idea of being rejected again, once the idea was planted there was no way she could ignore it.

Shimmying out of her clothes as quickly as possible—he had been in the shower for a while—she headed toward the bathroom. Toward Jesse. With a deep breath for courage, she slipped into the shower and let her hungry eyes wander over Jesse's strong body.

He was still beautiful to her. Decades of working with horses had honed his body into a well-oiled machine. The well-defined muscles of his back rippled with his every movement. She trailed a finger over his collarbone, down his chest, skimming across his flat stomach before drifting lower. She watched his body react to her touch, watched him grow hard under her fascinated gaze.

He grabbed her hand inches before she reached her goal.

Her gaze darted to his, and for a moment she was caught in their tortured midnight depths. His breathing was ragged, his body as fully aroused as her own. She knew how to inflame him, how to drive him beyond the rigid control he was so painfully exerting. But she had come this far—the next move was his. And so she waited, chest heaving, body tingling, for him to make a decision.

He stared into her eyes for long moments, his indecision plain to see. She was painfully aware of her nakedness and with every second that passed, her discomfort grew until she was shaking under the weight of her regrets. She'd made a horrible mistake in thinking that Jesse felt the same way. He didn't need her the way she needed him. He really was over her, despite the chemistry that still existed between them.

She started to apologize but there was nothing left to say. It really was too little, too late.

She lowered her head and turned to leave, regret and exhaustion dragging at her. Then he moved, one hand tugging her against him while his other hand thrust into her hair and pulled her head back for his kiss. He was starving, ravenous, completely out of control as his mouth ravished hers. He parted her lips without waiting for an invitation, his tongue sliding over and around hers. Tasting, testing, rediscovering all of her secrets.

And she let him, pressing herself against him, opening herself to him completely. This is what she'd craved for so long, what she'd needed all those lonely nights when she'd lain in bed waiting in vain for him to come to her. The passion, the connection, the sense of rightness that came only with being in his arms.

"I need you, Desiree," he muttered, his lips skimming over her cheek, down to the hollow of her throat, then lower. He cupped her breasts in his hands, bent his head and took a nipple into his mouth.

Desiree moaned, her hands clasping his head and locking him to her as she arched her back and offered herself to him. "I need you, too."

His tongue circled the hard bud again and again before he began to suckle her in a rhythm guaranteed to drive her completely out of her mind. "Please," she cried, her lower body moving restlessly against his.

He lifted his head for a moment, his grin darkly wicked as he surveyed her wild eyes and quivering body. "Please what?" he demanded, leaning forward and licking the hollow of her throat, his tongue stroking in rhythm to her pounding heart.

Desiree's knees buckled and she grabbed on to Jesse to keep from falling. "No more," she gasped, her hands clutching his shoulders tightly. "I need you inside me. Now."

He dropped to his knees in front of her, softly parting her silky folds. Before she could prepare herself, he'd leaned forward and thrust his tongue into her.

She screamed, her knees turning to jelly instantly. She would have fallen without the support of the wall behind her and Jesse's lithe strength in front of her. He held her pinned to the wall as he devoured her, his tongue stroking her from the inside out. Sensations bombarded her one after another—the cold tile behind her, Jesse's hot mouth on and inside her, the steaming water streaming over her. It was too much and she came, screaming Jesse's name as tears poured down her cheeks.

"I can't wait any longer," he muttered as he stood, lifting and pressing her against the wall in one smooth move.

"Wrap your legs around me," he ordered, and she complied, still desperate for him despite the mind-blowing release he had given her. His mouth captured hers and she tasted herself on his lips as need arrowed violently through her.

Jesse reached down, cupped her bottom in his huge, hot hands. "Now," he gasped, burying himself inside her with one powerful thrust.

She closed her eyes, completely overwhelmed with the sense of joy and rightness that came with having him inside of her after so long an absence. She wanted to stay like this forever, wrapped around him with no intention of ever letting go.

Then he moved, thrusting powerfully into her, and everything scattered, fading away until her entire reality was centered on Jesse and the incredible pleasure he was giving her. She moaned, her head thrashing restlessly against the shower wall as she met him thrust for thrust.

"Jesse, please—" she gasped, wrapping her arms around him and pulling him as close as she possibly could. "I can't take any more. I can't—"

He took her lips in a kiss designed to send her straight over the edge. At the same time, he slipped a hand between them and stroked her, once, twice. She exploded on the third pass of his thumb, her body arching against his as a violent release swept through her.

Jesse rode her through it, his body moving faster and faster against hers until, with a groan, he flooded her. His release went on and on, long and powerful.

Desiree watched Jesse return to himself, could tell the exact moment that everything came roaring back. The gleam in his eyes disappeared, as did the grin curving his mouth. With a grimace, he settled her feet back on the shower floor before turning away.

"Don't," she whispered as he reached for the soap.

"Don't what?" he asked remotely, as he lathered up a washcloth and began running it briskly over his body.

"Don't turn away from me. Not now, not yet."

His sigh was heavy as he stepped aside to let her take a turn under the cascading water. "We keep doing this."

"Doing what?" She stared at him, confused.

"Using sex to gloss over our problems. We've been doing it for years, Desiree, and it's held our marriage together despite our differences."

"Is that so bad?" She reached a tentative hand out to him, shocked when he actually let her touch him.

"It is when nothing gets solved. We're right back where we've been so many times before."

"It doesn't have to be like that."

"Doesn't it?" He sounded more tired than she had ever heard him. "I don't know what you want from me."

"I want to know how to fix this." She shut off the water then turned to face him, terror coursing through her as she laid everything on the line. "I want you to stay with me."

"It's a little late for this discussion, isn't it?" He handed her a towel before wrapping a second one around his waist and stepping out of the shower. "Months too late."

"I haven't signed the papers yet." She followed him into the bedroom, her pride gone as she all but pleaded with him. "And I won't until we have a chance to talk about this."

"What's there to talk about? We're on two different paths going in two different directions."

"That's not true." She wouldn't let it be true.

"Give me a break. We're so out of touch with each other that you didn't even know I was thinking about a divorce."

"That's because you never said anything about it." Her voice rose despite her best intentions. "You never even mentioned it to me until after you'd given me the papers."

"I thought moving out of our bedroom was a pretty good indicator that I wasn't happy."

"Why did you do that?"

He stared at her in disbelief. "You're asking me that now?"

"Yes."

"What does it matter? It's too late."

"It matters to me." Her voice was steady, her eyes calm. "It's always mattered to me."

"Which is why you never so much as mentioned it before today, right? Because it mattered so much to you?"

She took a deep breath, bit the proverbial bullet. "I was too scared to ask you before."

"Scared?" he demanded. "Of what?"

"Of finding out how badly I'd failed you. Of hearing you list all the reasons you don't love me anymore." She didn't try to hide her pain from him. There'd already been too much hiding. If he left her tomorrow, he would do so knowing how much she still loved him.

"It's never been about whether or not I loved you, Desiree."

"Then what was it about? What made you move out of our room? What made you file for divorce just when I'd begun to realize my mistakes and try to fix them?"

"What exactly have you been trying to fix?"

She stiffened at his tone. "A hell of a lot, but I guess you've been too busy to notice."

Jesse reached for a pair of boxers and a T-shirt, shaking his head as he did so. "That's the best you've got, huh?"

"How is it that you can make me angrier than any other person on earth?"

"I don't know. But I think that's a pretty good sign that we aren't meant to be together."

"Don't say that." She clutched at him but he pulled away.

"What do you want me to say?"

"I—"

"What, Desiree? Tell me what you want me to do, because I can't live like this anymore."

"I want you to love me." The words broke the dam on the emotions she'd held inside for so long. "I want you to let me love you, to let me make the past few years up to you.

"I want a second chance, or a third or a fourth chance. Whatever chance I'm up to by now, I want it. I want to focus on you for a change, on us, instead of on this stupid ranch. I want to go on a second honeymoon, where we can talk and lie on the beach and make love all day if that's what we want to do.

"I want to get to know you again. I want you to get to know me. I want you to look at me and see your wife again. I want to prove to you that I've changed, prove that you mean more to me than anything ever has. I want you to hold me like you used to, to kiss me and hug me and tell me that everything's going to be all right. Even if it isn't. Especially if it isn't. I want you to love me and I'm scared, so scared, that you'll never be able to again."

JESSE FELT HIS MOUTH FALL open but couldn't close it for the life of him. He hadn't seen Desiree this way since her mother died—hysterical, incoherent, completely devastated as she poured her heart out to him.

He crossed to her before he could remind himself what a damn fool he was to fall into this trap again.

"Stop, darlin'." He crooned the words as he pulled her into his arms, her body flush against his. "Please, stop. You'll make yourself sick."

Her shoulders continued to shake, her body shuddering with her grief. "I hired a new trainer so that you could have more time to spend on your line. You'd always be in charge but I thought Tom could take over some of the less important stuff that you do so that you could concentrate on Cherokee Dreaming. I know it's your dream just as I know you've put it on hold over and over again through the years for the Triple H, for me."

He stiffened against her, but she was too caught up in her words and her misery to notice. "I hired someone to help Bob out, thought that maybe I could put some of my responsibilities on him so that we could spend more time together. I had papers drawn up making you a partner in the ranch. Fifty-fifty."

"Desiree, stop it." His voice was low and shaky as shock after shock reverberated through him.

"No. I won't stop. I've held this inside for a long time and I'm sick of it. Sick of hiding behind my pride and pretending that your disinterest isn't killing me." She reached up, her hands tangling in his hair as she looked him in the eye. "I know what you've done for me, what you've done for this ranch. Don't think for one second that I don't know where we'd be if Big John hadn't hired you, if you hadn't stayed on after we got married, though you didn't want to. Without you we'd be a hell of a lot less than what we are. *I'd* be a hell of a lot less."

She brought her lips to his and he tasted the saltiness of her tears along with the wild sweetness that had always been a part of her. "I know I've screwed up. I've made mistakes with you, treated you carelessly. But there is one truth that you have to know, that you can't ever doubt." Her hands clenched in his hair as she stared into his eyes, her own now mercifully dry and filled with conviction. "I love you, Jesse Rainwater. I've loved you since I was sixteen years old and I will love you until the day I die. Marriage or no marriage. Divorce or no divorce. You will always be the only man I have ever loved."

He stared at her for a long time, his own pain obvious even as he shook his head. "It's too late, Desiree."

"Why is it too late? I still love you and you still love me." Her eyes met his. "You do still love me, don't you?"

"I told you, it's not about love."

"Of course it is. If we love each other—"

"Are you really that naive?"

"What do you mean?"

"We've always loved each other, darlin'. For thirty-two years, I've loved you and I know you've felt the same way about me."

"I have, Jesse, I—"

He held up a hand. "But too many things have been said, Desiree. Things that can't be taken back. We're just not good for each other."

He cupped her cheek in his hand, brushing tenderly at the unending line of tears with his thumb. "I love you, but I can't live like this anymore. I won't live like this anymore."

"It won't be like this anymore. I've changed—"

"It's not all you, darlin'. You've told me everything you've done wrong, but you left out all the mistakes I've made along the way."

Her eyes widened in shock and he cursed himself. He'd been such an ass these past two years that it had never occurred to her that he could recognize his own mistakes, as well. "For twenty-seven years it's bothered me that you wouldn't let me make a home for us away from here. It's made me bitter, made me feel inferior because I was living here, off of you."

"Jesse, no!"

"I got so caught up in the emasculation I felt at not providing for you that I let it drive a wedge between us, a huge wedge that's gotten bigger and deeper as the years have passed. I thought I could live with it. When Rio was born, I told myself I *would* live with it. And I have. But I've never let the feelings go, never moved past it. And because it was such a big thing for me, I couldn't believe that it wasn't just as huge for you."

"Jesse, your contributions to this ranch and this family are huge. I've never doubted that."

He nodded, smiling sadly. "I know that…now. Just like I know you've never thought about it the same way I did. But I can't get past it in my own head. Even now, with our marriage destroyed, I can't get past it. It's broken me, Desi. It's broken us and I don't see how we can be put back together."

"I can't accept that." The tears were gone and in their place was the determination he knew so well.

"I don't think you have a choice."

"The hell I don't. We can still fix this."

He shook his head. "I thought you'd hired Tom to replace me."

"Jesse, no." Her eyes were wide and shocked. "You couldn't have."

"I did. That's what I mean, darlin'. There's no trust left between us. I go through life expecting you to hurt me and you do the same. That's not a marriage."

"So you're just going to give up? Run away?"

He stiffened. "I'm not running away."

"What would you call it?"

He shrugged. "Strategic disengagement."

"What is this—a war?"

"It has been, for a very long time. And I'm tired. I can't fight anymore."

"So you're going to quit on us?"

"I don't know what else to do."

"Help me fix what's wrong."

"How, Desiree? I can't wave a magic wand and win the Triple Crown for you."

"Maybe it's not meant to be won."

It was his turn to stare at her. "What did you just say?"

She shrugged. "Forty years is a long time to go without a winner. Maybe there's a reason for that."

He shoved a hand through his hair as he continued to stare, openmouthed, at her. "Are you kidding me?"

"Do you really think that stupid prize is more important to me than you?"

"It's been the most important thing in your life for more than twenty years, Desiree. That doesn't change overnight."

"It is when I'm hit between the eyes with a sledgehammer." She held her hand up as he began to speak. "But, to be honest, I've spent the past year figuring out that trying to prove myself to a dead man is useless. It's worse than useless and it certainly isn't worth our marriage."

"You don't mean that."

"I do mean it."

He shook his head in disbelief. "Until next year, when we lose the Derby or the Preakness."

"No." She shook her head.

"Yes. I know you too well."

"No, you don't. If you did, we wouldn't be here now, facing the end of our marriage."

"Desiree—"

"Jesse." She reached out, grasped both his arms and waited until he was looking into her eyes. "I can't prove any of this to you. You're going to have to trust me."

"Isn't that what we've been talking about? Trust isn't exactly our long suit."

She let him go, slowly folding her arms over her chest as the truth sank in. "So that's it, then? We're finished?" She began gathering her clothes, her spine stiff, her movements jerky.

He searched within himself for words that could express the fear and hope battling inside of him. She'd hurt him so many times before that part of him thought it was suicide to give her another chance to destroy him. They'd wandered so far from where they'd started that it was hard to imagine finding a way back to what they'd once had.

And yet, could he really turn her down when everything inside of him called out for her?

"Don't leave me." The words tumbled out, unbidden. They weren't what he'd planned to say, but as Desiree froze in midmotion, he realized he didn't want to take them back.

She turned to face him. "What did you say?"

"Please, don't go." He took his first steps toward

her. "I'm not sure where we go from here, not sure if we can fix all the hurt we've inflicted on each other through the years. But I don't want to be without you. Not yet."

"Yes," she murmured, throwing her arms around his neck and holding on. "God, yes."

"But I do think you were right. We need to get away from the ranch for a while, spend some time figuring things out without all the angst and pain the Triple H has been about for so long."

She started to speak, but he interrupted her. "And I want you to tear up the partnership papers."

"But I thought that's what you wanted."

"What I wanted was to feel like my wife understood and appreciated me."

"I've always appreciated you, Jess, though understanding is something I'm just now working toward."

"We'll work toward it together. Tom was telling me about this counselor that saved his and Maureen's marriage."

She stared at him, surprised. "You want to go to counseling?"

"I think we need something if we're going to have any kind of chance at all. We've known each other for thirty-five years and I think we understand each other less now than we ever have before."

"But that's going to change." Her eyes were bright with a hope he hadn't seen in far too long.

"I don't know if it will or not." His voice was resolute, daring her to take a leap of faith. "But I want it to."

"Then that's good enough for now."

* * * * *

Here is a sneak preview of
A STONE CREEK CHRISTMAS,
the latest in Linda Lael Miller's acclaimed
MᴄKETTRICK *series.*

A lonely horse brought vet Olivia O'Ballivan
to Tanner Quinn's farm, but it's the rancher's
love that might cause her to stay.

A STONE CREEK CHRISTMAS
Available December 2008
from Silhouette Special Edition.

Tanner heard the rig roll in around sunset. Smiling, he wandered to the window. Watched as Olivia O'Ballivan climbed out of her Suburban, flung one defiant glance toward the house and started for the barn, the golden retriever trotting along behind her.

Taking his coat and hat down from the peg next to the back door, he put them on and went outside. He was used to being alone, even liked it, but keeping company with Doc O'Ballivan, bristly though she sometimes was, would provide a welcome diversion.

He gave her time to reach the horse Butterpie's stall, then walked into the barn.

The golden retriever came to greet him, all wagging tail and melting brown eyes, and he bent to stroke her soft, sturdy back. "Hey, there, dog," he said.

Sure enough, Olivia was in the stall, brushing Butterpie down and talking to her in a soft, soothing voice that touched something private inside Tanner and made him want to turn on one heel and beat it back to the house.

He'd be damned if he'd do it, though.

This was *his* ranch, *his* barn. Well-intentioned as she was, *Olivia* was the trespasser here, not him.

"She's still very upset," Olivia told him, without turning to look at him or slowing down with the brush.

Shiloh, always an easy horse to get along with, stood contentedly in his own stall, munching away on the feed Tanner had given him earlier. Butterpie, he noted, hadn't touched her supper as far as he could tell.

"Do you know anything at all about horses, Mr. Quinn?" Olivia asked.

He leaned against the stall door, the way he had the day before, and grinned. He'd practically been raised on horseback; he and Tessa had grown up on their grandmother's farm in the Texas hill country, after their folks divorced and went their separate ways, both of them too busy to bother with a couple of kids. "A few things," he said. "And I mean to call you Olivia, so you might as well return the favor and address me by my first name."

He watched as she took that in, dealt with it, decided on an approach. He'd have to wait and see what that turned out to be, but he didn't mind. It was a pleasure just watching Olivia O'Ballivan grooming a horse.

"All right, *Tanner,*" she said. "This barn is a disgrace. When are you going to have the roof fixed? If it snows again, the hay will get wet and probably mold…"

He chuckled, shifted a little. He'd have a crew out there the following Monday morning to replace the roof and shore up the walls—he'd made the arrangements over a week before—but he felt no particular compunction to explain that. He was enjoying her ire too much; it made her color rise and her hair fly when she turned her head, and the faster breathing made her perfect breasts go up and down in an enticing rhythm. "What makes you so sure I'm a greenhorn?" he asked mildly, still leaning on the gate.

At last she looked straight at him, but she didn't move from Butterpie's side. "Your hat, your boots—that fancy red truck you drive. I'll bet it's customized."

Tanner grinned. Adjusted his hat. "Are you telling me real cowboys don't drive red trucks?"

"There are lots of trucks around here," she said. "Some of them are red, and some of them are new. And *all* of them are splattered with mud or manure or both."

"Maybe I ought to put in a car wash, then," he teased. "Sounds like there's a market for one. Might be a good investment."

She softened, though not significantly, and spared him a cautious half smile, full of questions she probably wouldn't ask. "There's a good car wash in Indian Rock," she informed him. "People go there. It's only forty miles."

"Oh," he said with just a hint of mockery. "*Only* forty miles. Well, then. Guess I'd better dirty up my truck if I want to be taken seriously in these here parts. Scuff up my boots a bit, too, and maybe stomp on my hat a couple of times."

Her cheeks went a fetching shade of pink. "You are twisting what I said," she told him, brushing Butterpie again, her touch gentle but sure. "I meant…"

Tanner envied that little horse. Wished he had a furry hide, so he'd need brushing, too.

"You *meant* that I'm not a real cowboy," he said. "And you could be right. I've spent a lot of time on construction sites over the last few years, or in meetings where a hat and boots wouldn't be appropriate. Instead of digging out my old gear, once I decided to take this job, I just bought new."

"I bet you don't even *have* any old gear," she challenged, but she was smiling, albeit cautiously, as though she might withdraw into a disapproving frown at any second.

He took off his hat, extended it to her. "Here," he teased. "Rub that around in the muck until it suits you."

She laughed, and the sound—well, it caused a powerful and wholly unexpected shift inside him. Scared the hell out of him and, paradoxically, made him yearn to hear it again.

* * * * *

*Discover how this rugged rancher's wanderlust is
tamed in time for a merry Christmas, in
A STONE CREEK CHRISTMAS.
In stores December 2008.*

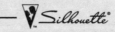

SPECIAL EDITION™

FROM *NEW YORK TIMES* BESTSELLING AUTHOR

LINDA LAEL MILLER

A STONE CREEK CHRISTMAS

Veterinarian Olivia O'Ballivan finds the animals in Stone Creek playing Cupid between her and Tanner Quinn. Even Tanner's daughter, Sophie, is eager to play matchmaker. With everyone conspiring against them and the holiday season fast approaching, Tanner and Olivia may just get everything they want for Christmas after all!

*Available December 2008
wherever books are sold.*

REQUEST YOUR FREE BOOKS!

2 FREE NOVELS PLUS 2 FREE GIFTS!

HARLEQUIN®

Super Romance®

Exciting, emotional, unexpected!

YES! Please send me 2 FREE Harlequin Superromance® novels and my 2 FREE gifts (gifts are worth about $10). After receiving them, if I don't wish to receive any more books, I can return the shipping statement marked "cancel." If I don't cancel, I will receive 6 brand-new novels every month and be billed just $4.69 per book in the U.S. or $5.24 per book in Canada, plus 25¢ shipping and handling per book and applicable taxes, if any*. That's a savings of close to 15% off the cover price! I understand that accepting the 2 free books and gifts places me under no obligation to buy anything. I can always return a shipment and cancel at any time. Even if I never buy another book from Harlequin, the two free books and gifts are mine to keep forever.

135 HDN EEX7   336 HDN EEYK

Name   (PLEASE PRINT)

Address   Apt. #

City   State/Prov.   Zip/Postal Code

Signature (if under 18, a parent or guardian must sign)

Mail to the **Harlequin Reader Service:**
IN U.S.A.: P.O. Box 1867, Buffalo, NY 14240-1867
IN CANADA: P.O. Box 609, Fort Erie, Ontario L2A 5X3

Not valid to current subscribers of Harlequin Superromance books.

Want to try two free books from another line?
Call 1-800-873-8635 or visit www.morefreebooks.com.

* Terms and prices subject to change without notice. N.Y. residents add applicable sales tax. Canadian residents will be charged applicable provincial taxes and GST. Offer not valid in Quebec. This offer is limited to one order per household. All orders subject to approval. Credit or debit balances in a customer's account(s) may be offset by any other outstanding balance owed by or to the customer. Please allow 4 to 6 weeks for delivery. Offer available while quantities last.

Your Privacy: Harlequin is committed to protecting your privacy. Our Privacy Policy is available online at www.eHarlequin.com or upon request from the Reader Service. From time to time we make our lists of customers available to reputable third parties who may have a product or service of interest to you. If you would prefer we not share your name and address, please check here. ☐

HSR08F

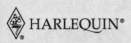

HARLEQUIN®

American ★ Romance®

HOLLY JACOBS
Once Upon a Christmas

Daniel McLean is thrilled to learn he
may be the father of Michelle Hamilton's
nephew. When Daniel starts to spend
time with Brandon and help her organize
Erie Elementary's big Christmas Fair, the
three discover a paternity test won't make
them a family, but the love they discover
just might....

***Available December 2008
wherever books are sold.***

LOVE, HOME & HAPPINESS

www.eHarlequin.com

HAR75242

#1530 A MAN TO RELY ON • Cindi Myers
Going Back

Scandal seems to follow Marisol Luna. And this trip home is no exception.
She's not staying long in this town that can't forget who she was. Then she
falls for Scott Redmond. Suddenly he's making her forget the gossip and
rethink her exit plan.

#1531 NO PLACE LIKE HOME • Margaret Watson
The McInnes Triplets

All Bree McInnes has to do is make it through the summer without anyone
discovering her secrets. But keeping a low profile turns out to be harder than
the single mom thought—especially when her sexy professor-boss begins to
fall in love. With her!

#1532 HIS ONLY DEFENSE • Carolyn McSparren
Count on a Cop

Cop rule number one: don't fall in love with a perp. Too bad Liz Gibson forgot
that one. Except unlike everybody else, she doesn't believe Jud Slaughter
killed his wife. Now she has to prove his innocence or lose him forever.

#1533 FOR THE SAKE OF THE CHILDREN • Cynthia Reese
You, Me & the Kids

Dana Wilson is *exactly* what Lissa thinks her single father needs. Dana is a
single mom *and* the new school nurse. Lissa's dad, Patrick Connor, is chair of
the board of education! Perfect? Well, there may be a few wrinkles that need
ironing out....

#1534 THE SON BETWEEN THEM • Molly O'Keefe
A Little Secret

Samantha Riggins keeps pulling J. D. Kronos back. With her he is a better
man and can forget his P.I. world. But when he discovers the secret she's been
hiding, nothing is the same. And now J.D. must choose between his former
life and a new one with Samantha.

#1535 MEANT FOR EACH OTHER • Lee Duran
Everlasting Love

Since the moment they met, Frankie has loved Johnny Davis. Yet their love
hasn't always been enough to make things work. Then Johnny is injured and
needs her. As she rushes to his side, Frankie discovers the true value of being
meant for each other.